THE HELPER OF THE FATHERLESS

THE WISE MAN AND THE WARRIOR BOOK 4

L.A. GOODYEAR

Publishing Coordinator – Sharon Kizziah-Holmes
Cover Design – Jaycee DeLorenzo

Paperback-Press
an imprint of A & S Publishing
A & S Holmes, Inc.

ISBN -13: 978-1-960499-83-7

DEDICATION

Maybe I jumped the gun in dedicating Book 2 to the fatherless, since that seems to be the obvious choice here! Oh well, I never claimed I was good at this. Could say it's dedicated to the HELPER of the fatherless. In a way it's true, but since all I do is dedicated to the Lord who saved me, there's nothing extraordinary about that.

How about this? I dedicate this book to the bride of the Lord Jesus Christ, the true Church He has built. In these days preceding the upward call to meet Him in the air, He is manifesting a divine split between His own beloved and the counterfeit church that has blended itself into it. He declared the angels would go forth just before harvest to bind the tares together for burning, then gather the wheat into His barn. The words and conduct of the people determine the camp into which they fall.

The closer one gets to thorns, the greater the chance of getting hurt. A religious spirit continuously speaks evil of the harmless while demanding they draw nearer, exposing themselves to more harm as they do! It reminds me of a lovesick porcupine. *"Forsake not the gathering of yourselves together, as is the manner of some ..."* The scripture is true, but sometimes leaving a particular gathering behind is a matter of self-preservation!

Jesus said, *"whatever you bind on earth will be bound in heaven, and whatever you loose on earth will be loosed in heaven."* He was talking about His Church at the time, so I'm not taking His words out of context. If you have to depart from a congregation, don't go it alone! The devil is looking for those so exposed, according to Peter. Bind yourself to others you KNOW live for Jesus, even if it's just one or two.

The Lord is in your midst, remember? He'll bring more to you as the days get darker. Take care of each other as refugees in Christ; that's the love He told us we're to share. It may look ragtag to you, but it's beautiful in His sight! This is the bride He's coming for, without spot, wrinkle or blemish. His eye is on those who follow Him in repentant sincerity. Academic excellence carries no weight with Him without repentance. Fellowship with Him is what He values, not head knowledge. If you don't know Him personally, all the other things you know won't help gain admittance into Heaven. Hell will have no shortage of doctorates.

-- L. A. Goodyear

ACKNOWLEDGMENTS

Paperback Press' proprietor **Sharon Kizziah-Holmes** works magic to get my stories in print, or so it seems to me! I am a published author because of her. That's no exaggeration. I'm not a household name yet, but the finished works my readers can hold in their hands are in no way inferior to products sold in bookstores everywhere and compare favorably to many of them. Her expertise gives my works that polish! Thanks again, Sharon.

Jaycee DeLorenzo made this cover. The lady is truly gifted. Whatever I ask for, she rises to the occasion every time. Sharon originally brought her on board for my first book, *Courtship of a Session Wrestler*, benefiting me by their association, but she has displayed resourcefulness ever since that excites me every time I work with her. I highly recommend her Sweet 'n Spicy Designs to anyone needing cover art.

My niece **Kimberly** took on the task of editing, this time. It's tedious work I can't do without, but she took it on despite holding a full-time job. In her shoes, I wouldn't have the energy. Thanks so much, Kim!

At 81, **my mom** is still at the forefront of those cheering me on. Can't let her down! She is the inspiration for Ruth in my ongoing story, if you've wondered. It wouldn't have come this far without her encouragement. Turning a daydream into print others can enjoy is a lot of work; it requires motivation and exhortation that can only come from outside one's self. She is a dependable source of the latter. Thanks, Mom!

As for the motivation ... If making money was the goal, my publishing adventure has been a colossal failure, so far. Continuing on this track would be utter folly, but there's much more to it than a hope of profit. The daydream may be therapeutic for me, but it doesn't need to be published to accomplish that goal. Keeping it to myself would actually avoid risk, since anything going public inevitably draws trolls!

God has given me the heart to share what is in me with strangers, in spite of the risk. You can't touch others when you remain out of reach yourself. Facades are a natural defense people hide behind, but this is their great failing. Ephesians tells us to put on the whole armor of God instead, making us mobile, enabling us to go to the hurting and comfort them wherever we find them. I hope my writings will comfort some of you out there. Even though it's fiction, the God of the Bible portrayed in it is not. He is the remedy for every affliction, now more than ever!

WHAT HAS GONE BEFORE, BOOK 2

Allen is a man struggling with rejection at the beginning of Book 1, *Courtship of a Session Wrestler*. His 38-year marriage had ended in divorce, rendering his life meaningless in his own eyes. God had a plan, though. Erin dreamed of a man she did not know for years until crossing paths with Allen during a cross-country trip. Just about as different as two people can be, love beyond explanation drew them together to become a couple others could rely on.

Their courtship and the events that followed made for an ongoing adventure. Allen's faith in God was time-tested and solid, but his self-confidence was shaken by the divorce. Erin is a pro wrestler brimming with confidence from a career of defeating men bigger than she is! Her dreams revealed his tenderness to her, moving her to respond to him the same way. Love isn't all they share. Christ's salvation message took root in her heart, when she chose to believe in Him.

Book 2, *The Battles That Matter*, has the retired couple living in Missouri with his widowed mother, Ruth. Erin, who was orphaned growing up, is delighted to have Mom with them! The wrestling business she owns is in Los Angeles, ran day-to-day by Erin's business partner, Stefanie. Though Erin retired to Missouri, she has a car in L.A. she needs to retrieve, so the newlyweds travel to California. They meet the lady wrestlers the business employs. Typically victorious over guys on the mats, they nevertheless struggle with life's baggage, some of which seems overwhelming.

The Lord enables Allen and Erin to minister to some of the young ladies in unique, personal ways. Allen is also assaulted, but God turns attempted murder into outright deliverance in front of everyone! Two receive Christ on the spot and their lives become entwined with the couple.

In Book 3, *War and Peace*, a grappler's new boyfriend challenges the company's reputation. Erin personally answers the challenge to put him in his place in a hilarious confrontation, leaving no question these ladies know their business! As more turn to Christ, events take place that serve notice the growing family of believers face supernatural opposition. He preserves His household without anyone getting hurt as only He can, even adding two established believers to their number who were looking for a church to join.

Finally, two major events were planned in the course of the story. These are detailed in the book you are about to read. I hope you find they were worth the wait. All this and more is ahead of you in Book 4, *The Helper of the Fatherless*!

CHAPTER 1

As they slept, Allen dreamed of the most beautiful white and gold wedding cake he had ever seen. The three tiers were a work of art. While he gazed in utter amazement, bees began to swarm. It became encrusted with the little insects, making it impossible to approach, much less try to cut a piece. The next morning, there was no unease associated with the dream, but it remained fresh in his mind.

Allen told Erin what he saw. She suggested it might be a warning about another Satanic attack. "Perhaps," he conceded. The plan was to set the cake on a table outside, easily accessible to all after the ceremony. He wondered aloud if they ought to keep it inside, just in case. She stated it was doable, though less convenient. They prayed briefly, receiving nothing but peace, so he was inclined to dismiss the dream.

Juanita overheard the discussion and pressed him for details. She had an idea. "Mr. Allen, when Gui gets here with the cake, he'll come in to find out where we want it.

You go out to look at it, okay? If it's like in your dream, then it came from God and he should bring it in the house; if not, it can be put outside." The plan seemed reasonable.

Unbeknownst to the couple, Juanita contacted Carlos to tell him what Allen saw as he slept. He called his brother, who was on his way in the bakery van. Whatever he told Guillermo really got his attention! When he rang the doorbell, he immediately asked to see Allen.

Allen's first impression was the younger man was likable, a stickler for details, maybe even a perfectionist. Where Carlos was slender and bookish, almost gangly, Gui was a little shorter and heavier, slightly older than Juanita. There was an air of impishness about him, like he might be about to pull a prank, but he was serious when he faced Allen.

After introductions were made, he asked for a description of the cake in the dream. As he received it, the color drained from the baker's face. He led him to the van, Erin, Juanita and Laurie accompanying them, then opened the side door. Gasps went up from the ladies as they took in his handiwork!

Allen nodded, "Yep, that's what I saw!" Suddenly looking sick, Guillermo turned away, bent over and prepared to vomit. "Can we pray for you, Gui?" he asked as Juanita offered her hand. He took it, nodding quickly.

As they joined hands, Allen spoke clearly, "In Jesus' holy name, Satan, desist! You are bound from causing any problems while you are here. Be still and silent!"

They began to pray. Gui gave him an odd questioning look until he noticed his involuntary retching had stopped. He seemed puzzled as he slowly straightened. They finished praying, thanked the Lord and asked the baker how he felt.

A broad smile spread over his face, "*That* never happened before. When my ulcer flares up, I'm usually sick for hours! Thanks, all of you!" Allen shook his head slightly, caught Erin watching, then shook it again in her sight. She nodded in understanding.

Juanita told Guillermo, "Jesus answered our prayer, Gui. You doing better now?"

He took stock of himself, then nodded an affirmative. "Yeah, much better! I think I can go through with this now." Laurie grinned.

Juanita latched onto her future brother-in-law. "I'm glad! It wouldn't be the same without you."

He looked at Allen as though trying to figure out what made him tick. "I think we better put the cake in the house, just to be safe. If God gave you a sneak peek at it for real, we *don't* want to see the rest of your dream come true! Do you have a table set up for it?"

"Give us a minute," Erin said, "Ladies?" She hustled off with Laurie in tow.

Juanita hesitated before giving him a peck on the cheek. "Gui, the cake is beautiful! Thank you so much!" she declared, then ran in pursuit of the other two. He was beaming at the praise.

Allen added, "It really is. I've never seen anything like it!"

He turned to him, "Until last night, I guess. Allen, I created a special honey glaze just for this cake. I envisioned a milk and honey look for it from the time my brother asked me to design something for them. It's an original; I've never used it before. I was so proud of how it turned out! The idea it might draw bees never crossed my mind. Maybe some testing is in order, but this isn't the time or place to do it. We can't risk ruining their wedding, can we?" he grinned.

Allen agreed. "Maybe a smaller test could be planned to see how bees respond to your glaze, where no one will get hurt," he suggested. Gui looked thoughtful.

Laurie stood in the doorway. "Guys, we're ready. Bring it to the reception room, okay?" They did, the two of them carefully navigating through the house, while the ladies opened doors and ensured the path was clear. Once in place, it drew people rather than bees, with oohs and aahs galore! It's a good thing photos aren't damaging to cake, or it would have been a puddle on the floor in no time!

Stef was the first to show up dressed for the ceremony, bringing in boxes of sausage biscuits, ham muffins, bagels and breakfast burritos. Those who were at the house all night ate gratefully, then went to get dressed. Stef showed Gui to her office so he could change.

In the privacy of their room, Erin stated, "That wasn't an ulcer making him sick."

"No," Allen confirmed, "it was the demon, realizing the power of God is working here. It wanted to get him away, afraid he might be set free."

"Will he, love?" she grinned hopefully.

He shrugged, "That's up to Guillermo. He has to accept the truth before he can be set free, then decide whether to receive Christ. Right now, he still believes an ulcer caused his trouble."

She deflated until he pointed out, "He knows God did something for him, Genie, at our request. He *has* to be mulling it over, extraordinary as it is. He loves Carlos and Juanita. I'm sure he's heard what the Lord's done for them – and He's not done yet! Give it time. God *always* finishes what He starts." Grinning again, she nodded, encouraged.

The ceremony was scheduled for 10:30 a.m. When Erin and Allen finished getting dressed, they found most of the staff had arrived. Reina was there and kept looking at him funny, but didn't stop to talk. He thought she must've heard what happened from Guillermo or Juanita.

She and Stef were coordinating the enthusiastic staff in preparations for the other guests. The airbrushed sign was placed in the front yard, pointing new arrivals to the gate opening into the backyard. In addition, two ladies were stationed up front to direct incoming foot traffic. Half a block away was a complex of medical offices that closed on weekends. Erin had obtained permission to use their parking lot.

Just inside the gate, Andrew and Delilah invited new arrivals to sign the guest book. Three more staff acted as ushers. Allen marveled at the way it was so organized, but Erin reminded him with a grin she had promised to set things up right, if he would do this. Henry, a camera operator, was even providing rides from the parking area down the street to the front yard!

Allen didn't know whether to greet people at the gate or not. Ministers typically do, but it seemed presumptuous to him, since he didn't meet the standard criteria. Carlos arrived and took the task on himself, saying he didn't want Allen disrespected. As the groom, no one could question his right to be there!

Grateful, Allen went in to be alone and pray. Some might consider him stuck up, but no matter what he did, there would be critics, so it seemed best to focus on the Lord. He did not know until he came out of the bedroom that Danielle posted herself by the door like a sentry. It startled him, making both of them laugh. She said Erin asked her to make sure he wasn't disturbed. He thanked Dani as they went out for the ceremony.

Two cameras were designated to record the event. When Henry arrived to man his, little Alissa brought the assemblage to order masterfully with her keyboard. She drew double takes from the crowd, first for her playing, second when they noticed her youth. When the music ended, Allen introduced himself by name without any title, just as a servant of Christ Jesus and friend of the couple. Some wondering looks gazed back at him, plainly curious about who he was. He let them wonder as the wedding march sounded, snapping their heads around.

Juanita was breathtaking on the elbow of her father. He strutted like a peacock, obviously proud of his daughter, to hand her off to Carlos. They approached the front and stopped. As Allen spoke again, his voice took on a volume he didn't know he could manage.

"Please bow your heads for a moment of prayer. *Father in heaven, this assemblage and these proceedings serve no purpose at all, unless You take notice to favor us with Your presence. You know these two souls standing before Your servant, because two weeks ago they repented of their sins and gave their hearts to You via the atonement You provided in Your faithful Son, Jesus our Lord, blessed forever.*

"*They have determined to put Your will ahead of their own, whatever the cost, just as our Lord did. They hope to do so together, strengthening one another. As they make this commitment today in Your sight before all these witnesses, I ask that You smile upon them as they seek to honor You and pour out Your blessing upon them, in Jesus' holy name. Amen.*"

For a brief moment, there was silence. Suddenly a mighty wind shook all the surrounding trees with such ferocity that those seated looked up in alarm, fearing a tornado had touched down! It didn't last, though, and the air around those gathered never stirred at all. Peace settled palpably where the wedding party stood, radiating outward.

There was no question they were being visited by an utterly awesome Presence, and no mistaking His pleasure and goodwill! It reflected on the faces of those present. Fear was banished, replaced with smiles coming from the joy He exuded.

CHAPTER 2

A hushed audience listened as Allen set forth how the couple received Christ. Recognizing their previous union did not honor Him or each other, they resolved together to start over. He pointed out how their resolution led to abstinence for a time, proving their commitment to righteousness was much more than lip service.

The Lord's presence was *resounding* evidence He had taken notice. His satisfaction was undeniable! The crowd barely moved. There wasn't even the usual fidgeting found in a seated gathering.

Allen turned his attention to the two before him, who seemed awestruck. He chuckled to loosen them up, "Do you think He noticed you?" They nodded together, their eyes wide and holding each other's hand, without a word. "When you offer Him a sacrifice, it doesn't escape His notice. He'd still be present, even without this manifestation, but you honored Him, so it pleased Him to honor you! Do we serve an awesome God, or what?"

Giggling, they nodded. Catching hold of the best man

and the matron, laughter spread across the crowd like a wave. It broke the tension of the stillness, made it okay to move, though the reverent silence held.

He led them in exchanging vows, though he stumbled once when addressing Juanita. Trying to correct it, he came out sounding like Porky Pig, stammering badly. He flushed and stopped a moment, embarrassed as he tried to recover. His eye caught Laurie's. Their gaze locked and he remembered his instruction to her. Laughing aloud at himself, he announced loudly, "Oops!" She nearly doubled over laughing. The crowd laughed, too, though not as hard.

Allen addressed Juanita. "I'm sorry, I messed up. Is it okay if I try again?"

She nodded, grinning. "You're doing great, Mr. Allen," she encouraged him.

Starting over, he got through it without further difficulty. Rings were produced and bestowed, then he made his final speech. "This is the part where someone usually says, 'By the power vested in me by the state of California, I now pronounce you man and wife.' It's not my place to say it, but it doesn't matter, because the state of California made the declaration when you stood before the judge last week, right?" They nodded emphatically, grinning.

He took their free hands and clasped them lightly. "Then I'll stick with the truth. By the trust I have received as a servant of the Most High God and a witness of the gospel of our Lord Jesus Christ, I declare this union valid, recognized in the kingdom of heaven, blessed in the sight of the King of kings and Lord of lords. Carlos, will you *please* kiss this extremely patient young lady?" Everyone cracked up, especially Juanita, even after the kiss.

If the Lord departed, no further unusual manifestations marked it. Allen made one final announcement, bringing a huge grin to Guillermo's face. "One last thing, folks. The best man created a wedding cake for these lovebirds that is truly a work of art. If you haven't seen it, you really should before it's cut. It's in the reception room in the house."

As the newlyweds commenced receiving the first of many congratulations, Allen felt very exposed, just for a moment. It didn't last. It was like he blinked and Erin was there, a small smile in place, shaking her head.

"I don't know how you do it, love! You are incredible to me!"

Then her arms were around him and he was complete once more. He wasn't alone and wasn't about to be. Their girls surrounded them, following up Erin's embrace with their own, expressing how beautiful they considered what they had seen. Laurie laughed, telling him she looked forward to the day he could marry her and her true love.

He stopped her short, "How? If I'm giving you away, won't I already be fulfilling my role?" When it sank in, she grinned. He nodded, "Uh-huh. Besides, I suspect I'll be too choked up to speak, anyway." A giggle accompanied another impulsive hug.

Their attention got pulled outward, as folks began to approach. Jorge, the bride's father, extended his hand. "Mr. Edwards, please accept my apology for doubting you. Two weddings, one to satisfy the state, another to honor God in heaven; I never heard of such a thing before, but this was exceptional."

A stern-looking woman beside him spoke. "It wasn't Catholic!" she declared, with a mix of anger and frustration.

"Be still!" he told her. Her mouth clapped shut. Jorge conceded, "No, it wasn't, but *she* isn't anymore, yet God attended their wedding. If He is pleased, would we oppose Him by objecting?" She shook her head, at a loss for words.

Allen replied, "Thank you. Without shame now, I think the two of them will be very happy together."

"Me, too," Jorge agreed. A little smile tweaked at the

corners of his wife's mouth as she glanced at her daughter, evidence she did care about her. That put a smile on Allen's face.

They turned away and Teresa, the matron of honor, was there, her face alight. "Allen, never in my life have I seen anything like this! I don't think any wedding from now on will measure up to my girl Juanita's. You've ruined them for me!" she laughed.

"When God shows up, it changes everything," he said. "All I do is serve Him."

With a nod, she acknowledged, "I get that. I have even more questions now. We *have* to talk. I'll be in touch." She bustled off before he could reply.

"My man!" Andrew towered before him grinning, his booming voice carrying over all the others in the yard. Allen stuck out his hand, but the big fellow shook his head, "No, that won't do at all!" He embraced Allen in a huge hug, yet very gentle, ever aware how easily his power could harm others, unintentionally. He returned the embrace the best he could, but his arms still didn't reach around his girth.

"You took me back to my roots today, Allen. When God showed up shaking the trees, it was like He shook me awake. I remembered in *detail* the meetings Mama took us to when we were kids. God was there, too! It impacted me so powerfully that I asked Jesus to come into my heart when I was just five. I had forgotten! It came back as you talked about Him, though. Does it still count with Him? I haven't lived for Him, but I never told Him to get lost, either. Where do I stand with Him now?"

Erin and their girls were watching and listening, but they weren't alone. Andrew's voice carried so two-thirds of those present heard him and went silent, waiting for the response. Andrew paid no attention, focused entirely on Allen.

"It matters, Andrew. It matters to God, or He wouldn't

have brought the memory back to mind. You made a commitment to Him with a child's faith, but your service to Him was limited by a child's attention span, so it didn't change how you lived. Still, it sensitized you to anything pertaining to Him, particularly His word and His presence.

"When you heard me quote His word the first time we met, it got your attention. When you felt His presence today, it brought all those memories back. Your heart is still His. If you had died up until now, you would have found yourself in His presence in heaven! Thanks to His grace and a simple child's act of faith, your sins were forgiven, even those committed since then, because you didn't know any better."

His eyes were brimming with tears, "Oh, wow! He remembered, even after I forgot!"

"*He* never forgets, Andrew. He loves you. He's not *about* to turn His back on you. You won't lose Him, unless you turn your back on Him. You gave Him a deposit on your undeveloped life. and now He's calling you on it.

"A child's faith kept you in His hand to this point, but it's time to decide if the man you've become will keep that child's promise. You heard a long time ago what Jesus did to redeem you. It moved you to repentance because you believed what you heard. *'Faith comes by hearing, and hearing by the Word of God.'* Do you still believe Him?"

"Y-yes - yes, I do, Allen. I remember that day like it was yesterday, even how I felt. I *meant* what I said to Him. I know now it carries a commitment to stop sinning, to put what He wants ahead of what I want. If He'll help me, I'll do it!"

Putting a hand on his shoulder, Allen guided him onto the faux grass carpet under the canopy. "Then bow with me and tell Him so, Andrew. The only thing changing is that you are replacing a child's faith with the intentionality of a grown man who has decided to live according to what he believes! You don't need me to lead you to Him, because you have already met Him and He has accepted you!"

Even in their suits, they went to their knees. Allen's hand remained on his shoulder as the big man dedicated his heart anew to Christ, sobbing. Praising the Lord, Allen closed his eyes, listening as his brother prayed, but they opened again by themselves. Crying, Erin and their girls were giving praise. A few steps away, Carlos and Juanita stood with Guillermo. The couple was grinning, while Gui's jaw was slack, his eyes wide.

He saw Delilah then, her lips pursed. He had an impression she was disgusted, then she wheeled and walked away. The crowd nearby was fixated, at a loss how to respond. A few looked sympathetic to the big man's sobs. Stef stood on the porch, gazing at them impassively. Nothing in her stance or expression indicated she was moved at all.

Andrew went quiet and looked up, "Allen, *thank you.* Mama's greatest wish was for me to know Christ, and now I do. I feel peace inside like never before! What should I do now?"

"Do you have a Bible?"

He nodded, "I have Mama's as a keepsake."

Allen shook his head, "It's more than that. It's a legacy and a cupboard full of food for your spirit. Ask God to feed you from it, to make it come alive, then immerse yourself in it! We have daily fellowship via conference call, where we share encouragement, pray, study the Bible, and visit. Erin will connect you," they glanced at her. She nodded.

"Andrew, there is one thing I can't underscore enough: *stay connected with us. Do not try to go it alone, understand?* The Devil is real, too, and aware of the commitment you just made to Christ. He hates Him and will make certain the decision you just made costs you. If you're not in close fellowship with other believers when it happens, it will feel like you have been gutted and left to die! Believe me, I'm not embellishing in the slightest.

"Satan is likened to a roaring lion, seeking whom he may devour, looking for stragglers and strays who wander off from the herd. Christ is the great Shepherd who stands guard over the sheep, but *we must stay near Him and each other*, lest we are exposed to our enemy. Reliance on Him and each other preserves us, but self-reliance will get us in over our heads before we know it!"

"I get you, Allen," he promised with a grin, "I'll stay in touch." They got to their feet. He looked around, "Anyone see Delilah?" Several pointed toward the house, so he lumbered away in pursuit.

Stef called out to the newlyweds, wanting to know if they were about ready to cut the cake. They told her, "In a minute," still being accosted by family members and guests. Guillermo wasn't there anymore. As Allen turned to meet Reina, movement caught his eye near the back gate into the alley. Gui was hurrying toward them, looking like something was on his mind. Reina saw him, too, and held off speaking as her younger son approached.

CHAPTER 3

"Oh good, Mom, you're here! I was coming to get Allen, but I want you all to see this." He gestured they should follow, then spoke again as they came to the back gate.

"I thought about what you said, Allen, and had an idea. When we deliver a cake, we carry a jar of frosting to make repairs, in case it gets bumped or scuffed during transit. Today, I brought a second jar with my new honey glaze, just to be safe. Before everyone got here, I took it into the alley and smeared a generous dollop on the telephone pole adjacent to the back fence. Now look!"

He opened the back gate and pointed. Across the alley, about five feet above the ground, little sparkles flashed in the sunlight, twinkling like tiny little lights. Upon closer scrutiny, it became apparent an area about the size of a softball had the glaze applied, but *honey bees covered nearly all of it!* Their tiny bodies blocked the light as they crawled all over it, allowing only momentary chinks of the shiny substance to reflect a sparkle before it was covered again! A chill ran down Allen's spine.

The baker looked directly at him. "Allen, my cake would have ruined the wedding if it had been placed outside! We need to talk."

He shuddered involuntarily. "Can we do it inside? This is creeping me out!" The ladies were in total agreement, and Reina was shivering. They wasted no time getting into the house.

Video footage was taken before and while the cake was cut. Space in the reception room allowed only a few to sit as they watched, but standing room permitted everyone a view. Gui took a bow for his handiwork, warning everyone the cake *must be eaten inside*, due to the unforeseen effect his honey glaze had in drawing bees. He apologized, but someone pointed out that beekeepers everywhere would have an interest in obtaining catnip for bees!

Curiosity moved those present to try the cake (as if they needed more motivation), which received rave reviews. It was consumed quickly, with punch and water. Sixty came in for cake; only eighteen left when the ceremony ended. Once they had a plate in hand, the dining room and living room accommodated the overflow until most of the guests left. Trash was double-bagged for the safety of those who took it out.

Staff was mobilized to help clean up, so it was over in no time. Reina prevailed in getting permission to take home the sign with the couple's airbrushed likeness, to her delight. Gui agreed to bring it in the van for her, however, she informed him she wasn't leaving yet. She wanted to hear the answers to his questions, citing she had some of her own.

Teresa also hung around. Allen expected she would need to get Alissa home, but the teen musician was in no hurry, curious about what they were going to discuss. His "entourage" stayed when the staff departed after the cleanup. Fran and Denise rounded out the number of those still present. Pam and Win hesitated, but said they'd talk later. They wanted to go home and change.

Gui seemed ready to burst as he kicked it off, "Allen, *where* did that dream of yours come from? It literally saved the wedding from becoming a disaster, and it would have been *my fault!*"

Allen recapped the dream for everyone present, which garnered wide-eyed expressions of surprise from most in the room, especially Alissa. He had wondered if it was good for her to be present for this. On asking the Lord about it, he received peace and decided to leave it in His hands. When Gui realized some present didn't know what happened, he told them of his experiment verifying the dream was based on truth. The baker wasn't the only one rattled!

Once everyone was clued in, Allen responded, "Gui, there is nothing special about me. That being true, I bet you can deduce the answer, rather than having to take my word for it.

"Who would know what your cake looked like without you showing Him, then be able to reveal its likeness to someone else, unveiling a liability it carried even *you* were unaware of? If more than one person is capable of this deed, who would *care* to prevent the disaster from happening? The dream came to me, you know. Whose servant have I proclaimed myself to be, openly before many witnesses today, yourself included?"

Smiles filled the room. Gui stated the obvious, a bit sheepishly, "God. Only God could do this and might want to save the wedding, might care enough about it. You said all the time you serve Him. You even led that big fellow, Andrew, to Him."

He shook his head. "I grew up Catholic, but I never saw God accomplish miracles before. Is this kind of thing ordinary for you? When my ulcer acted up, you prayed and the pain stopped, I was okay to keep going. Miracles were things I only heard about, until today. Now I've encountered three, counting the wind in the trees that didn't touch us. Your God is different from the one I've heard about. How?"

"Jesus Christ, the One written about in Matthew, Mark, Luke, and John, declared He is the way, the truth, and the life, and no one comes to the Father, except by Him. *No one* includes priests, cardinals, even the Pope, Gui. They can't make a connection with Him any more than we can, without first coming to Jesus.

"Addressing saints or Mary is worse than useless. Though unintentional by most worshippers, it's actually disobedient, because Jesus bade us to come to Him directly. He changes everything when we do! There is no substitute or intermediary for God's only begotten Son. The power of God is revealed in Him! I serve Him, so if you see the power of God operating in my life, you know He must be the Source."

A wry smile reflected on Reina's face, "I think you know that's heresy to a Catholic, Allen."

"Yes, ma'am, I know. But if it's true, then the Catholic Church is wrong, plain and simple. Jesus told us to come unto Him directly, yet Catholicism says you can't. *Somebody* is wrong, for sure. I side with Jesus, as do Carlos and his wife. That's why they're not Catholic anymore. You're deciding where you stand, or you wouldn't still be sitting here, would you?" She nodded with a grin, wordlessly.

"Did you hear about the attempt on my life, Gui?"

He nodded, "Yeah. The woman had a demon inside her?"

Alissa looked shocked. Allen gave her his full attention. "Alissa, I don't know your beliefs. I certainly don't want to scare you. Everyone else here has heard what happened to me, how Jesus saved my life, so I'm not going to recount the details right now, just for you. If you want, any of us can tell you about it later, okay?"

She nodded.

He cautioned her, "I can tell you, though, demons are real, just like God is, and I'm going to talk about them now. If you think you need to leave the room, go ahead. We understand."

She replied, "Mr. Edwards, I think I'll be okay. I'm nearly a grown-up. I'm curious, but I feel like I *need* to be here, somehow. Can I stay?"

The rest looked sympathetic. He told her, "The truth is the truth. Young people like you hear an awful lot that *isn't* true, so I think you should hear it, if you're ready. If Teresa is good with it, you can stay. You're her responsibility right now."

Teresa smiled at her, "If it gets to be too much, we'll both leave, okay?" Alissa gave a quick nod, then turned back to listen intently.

He returned his attention to Gui. "Yes, she did, but she didn't know it was a demon until it turned against her. It tried to kill her when it failed to kill me. I cast it out, under the authority of Jesus' name. She is free of it now. The thing is, she had been taught it was a wise entity that had ascended to a higher plane in ancient times. By sharing her life and body with it, she gained power and knowledge. It posed as something benevolent, when all it was doing was using her.

"This kind of deception is much more widespread than people know. Many in show business have been suckered into bondage by demons masquerading as something else. Stars label them as their muse or alter ego, and credit these separate 'personalities' as the ones with all the talent.

"It's not true, but they believe it is, so they rely on their alter ego because they believe their success is dependent on it. Like Clark Kent changing into Superman, they call up that 'superior version' of themselves when they want to excel, more and more as time goes by. They don't realize how they are giving up their own identity by their reliance, losing themselves in the process."

Guillermo looked flustered and excited all at once. "Allen, *I* have an alter ego, the real genius behind my creations. He's the one who created the honey glaze ..." he stopped, realizing what he was saying.

Allen finished his sentence, "...that almost ruined the wedding you wanted to be a part of, with nothing but good intentions. He sabotaged you, Gui! He's been lying to you all along. Your artistic genius is your own, a talent your Creator designed into you when he formed you in the womb.

"Think back to this morning, when we prayed for you. Your nausea came on when I recognized your cake and you were warned it could draw swarms of bees. Only God could give the warning, so the demon, your 'alter ego,' knew he was exposed. He tried to incapacitate you with your 'ulcer.' When I bound Satan from causing trouble, your retching stopped instantly, *before* we started praying for you. It wanted you away from here before you could be set free!"

Guillermo looked at him, thinking. "He's still here, but he's not responding to me. If he is a demon, why didn't you cast him out?"

"I couldn't, because you welcomed him. As long as you believe he is the best part of you, the last thing you'd want to do is lose him. To be free of deception, you need to hear the truth, accept it, and want to be free. Jesus doesn't force freedom on anyone. He respects our free will choices; otherwise, no one could reject Him."

Teresa spoke up, "So you're saying he has a demon, but it is bound? Is that permanent?"

He shook his head, "No, it's not. Do you remember the condition of my binding, Gui?"

He hesitated, but Juanita didn't. "I remember what you said, Mr. Allen. You bound Satan and told him to be silent, as long as Gui is here. He is not allowed to cause problems while he is here."

The baker looked up sharply. "So as soon as I leave, he'll be free again. That's why he's not responding to me now. This is kind of scary, Allen. If he's just a part of me, he should do what I want. You'd have no power over him. If you command him to come out of me and he leaves, then he must be a demon, right? I know my alter ego is there now - I can tell. Will I know when he's gone? How?"

"You'll know, I promise." Allen stood. "Gui, it is Jesus who will set you free if you want, but only He can keep you free. If you are not willing to repent of your sins and give your heart to Him, you're better off leaving now and keeping the demon. Jesus taught when a demon is cast out, he eventually returns. If he doesn't find Jesus living in you, he will move back in, bringing seven even more wicked demons with him! I don't want such an outcome for you. You need to go all the way with this, or not at all. What do *you* want?"

CHAPTER 4

Gui stepped up to him. "If the demon is real, Allen, then Jesus must be, too. It would have ruined my brother's wedding, maybe even got someone hurt. If that's intentional, it's not me and I want it gone!"

"It's done much worse to you than you know, brother," he replied. "You are about to have your eyes opened. Satan, in the name of Jesus of Nazareth, come out of him and begone." Nothing happened. Anger rose in Allen, but it wasn't his own. *"NOW!"* he thundered, placing his hand on Gui's forehead.

The baker began to convulse. Several voices began wailing in unison through his mouth until his head flung back toward the ceiling. Suddenly, he dropped to the floor like a marionette whose strings had been cut and laid there, gasping for breath. Reina dropped to her knees, crying, *"Dios Mio!"* as she watched her son.

He got to his knees, sweat clinging to his now pale skin, "Oh, Jesus, that filth was *inside* me! I did such horrible things with other men, because they wanted me to! Please forgive me, make me clean!"

A breeze flowed through the room carrying the freshest air, like no one had ever breathed it before. Teresa and Alissa went to their knees, asking forgiveness for their sins, breathing deeply of the cool, refreshing air, as did Reina. The rest went into tongues. Laying hands on the four of them, they also started speaking in foreign tongues. Guillermo wept long and hard as sorrows were washed clean with tears, while all of them thanked God and prayed in tongues.

They eventually wound down, thanking Jesus over and over for His grace in heeding their prayers. One or two would laugh, then someone else, like it was a relay. As the new believers stood, Reina embraced Gui and crowed, "My son has come home! Thank you, Jesus, for bringing us home!" Carlos and Juanita wrapped their arms around him, too. The three of them held him while he chuckled, absorbing the love.

Finally he told Reina with a grin, "Mom, you know I'm not moving home with you, don't you?"

She jabbed him in the ribs playfully, "You know what I mean, joker!"

Teresa cracked up. Alissa had the giggles. The prim young lady from before had vanished, replaced by a delighted girl who struggled to contain her joy. It got Laurie giggling, too. With a shrug, she embraced the youngster and they giggled together until they burst out laughing at themselves! All the girls took turns embracing her, welcoming her to the family of Christ, even their waitress friends.

Juanita released Gui to approach Teresa. "Well, Cuz, what do you think now? Still worried whether me and Carlos are on the right track with our new faith?"

Teresa blushed, glanced at Allen and chuckled, "Not anymore. You discovered what we were missing, the power of God found in Christ Jesus alone. Jesus Christ is *more* than the perfect martyr for righteousness, always depicted on a cross. He is the final victor over sin, longing to embrace whoever comes to Him and providing deliverance from every snare of the Devil. Like Guillermo, like all of you, I have come home to Him, following in *your* footsteps, girl. Thank you for showing me the way!" she seized Juanita and wept on her shoulder, which brought tears to the younger woman, also.

Reina turned loose of her son to approach Allen. "I just have one big disagreement with what you said, mister. You were wrong when you told Gui there is nothing special about you! You are unique, one-of-a-kind in how the love and nature of Jesus shines through you, and don't you forget it!"

Erin chuckled, her arm snaking around his waist to pull his hip against hers. "We all disagree with him on that point, Reina. If a vote was taken, he's aware he'd lose."

"Well, y'all are biased," he mumbled.

"Maybe a little," Erin admitted, "but you're nearsighted, in how you see yourself."

"Hey, Carlos," he called out to get his attention. He looked over and saw his smile. "Do you realize we're not the only guys in the family now?"

Carlos lit up, clapping Gui on the arm. "That's right! Mr. Allen and I are getting reinforcements, kind of, with you and Andrew!" It got the ladies laughing.

Allen began to share then, explaining the work of the Holy Spirit with the significance of His self-expression in foreign tongues. The others helped him describe how they sustain their faith through daily conference call Bible studies, also ensuring they don't drift apart. The new believers were excited to hear they were not aloof in their separate lives, as religious people often are.

Alissa was *thrilled*, revealing her family was very secular and intellectual. They would sneer if she tried to attend a church. She believed her newfound faith would isolate her, perhaps even draw ridicule. Her connection to this group would be her lifeline, she said. Teresa reminded her their connection through music predated the new faith she shared with Alissa now, so she also had that contact to help keep them connected.

For Allen, the thought of her feeling isolated brought someone else to mind. He resolved silently to ask Heidi if she would call the youngster, once she heard how Jesus saved his life. He had no doubt the curious teen would look into it, likely before the day ended!

The doorbell rang. It was the rental company, coming to pick up their things. Dani went out to watch. Erin whispered to Laurie and Emily, then all three left the room. Considering how protective they were of him, he was surprised all of them left his side, but decided they must have thought him safe in this group.

Dani rejoined him barely two minutes later, having been relieved by Erin after she changed clothes, apparently at breakneck speed. She was watching over him as closely as ever, he reflected wryly. A few minutes later, the other girls returned carrying plates of sandwiches for everyone, which were received gratefully. Erin settled down next to him as they returned with drinks.

He looked at her, shaking his head. "You are a marvel, you know?"

She grinned, "Hey, if I'm your Wonder Woman, I have a reputation to live up to, don't I?"

He replied in open admiration, "You're doing it, Genie, no question." She kissed his cheek and told him to eat his sandwich before his sugar dropped too low.

After eating, the bride and groom indicated they were getting ready to leave. They said they wouldn't be seeing anyone again until tomorrow, but wouldn't elaborate when Allen asked why, to the amusement of those present. Gui joined in, asking why they would want to leave, when they felt so loved and wanted among this group?

Laughing, Reina ushered them out the front door, telling them they'd see them tomorrow. They left smiling and laughing. Afterward, she turned to admonish Allen, "Do I need to tell you about the birds and the bees?"

He caught Alissa's eye and deliberately winked. "Reina, I'm not sure I'm old enough to hear about the facts of life. Isn't that stuff for grown-ups?" The teen cracked up, along with the rest, particularly his girls.

Erin spoke up with a chuckle, "He knows more than he's letting on, believe me."

He came right back, "Yeah, she's a good teacher. I was a virgin until she came along!" Howls of laughter and a slap on the shoulder in mock outrage rewarded his declaration.

"I thought you said you'd stick to the truth!" Erin reminded him.

"Oh, yeah, I said that during the ceremony, didn't I?" He hesitated, "Hey, Genie, you do know the ceremony is over now, don't you?" She shook her head in frustration, finally sticking her tongue out at him. Gui stated he was a man after his own heart.

Reina snorted, "That just means now there are two of them who are full of hot air!"

They laughed often as they continued to visit. Teresa must have been enjoying herself. Allen thought she might leave right after Juanita and Carlos did, but that wasn't the case. She wasn't just accommodating her teen charge, either. She laughed and visited as much as Alissa did, apparently quite comfortable with them. The Lord formed a bond to include their new brethren in heartfelt affection going both ways. This phenomenon always amazed Allen, causing him to appreciate Him even more.

Gui decided to change back to street clothes, which got others talking about how nice it would be to do the same. Fran let it be known she had a date for the evening, but asked how long Erin and Allen would be in town, hoping to see them again. They planned to fly home Monday, giving them the weekend before their departure. She promised she would see them tomorrow, then left.

Denise said she'd like to hang with the group, if it was okay. The girls called her over and sat her in their midst, informing her she was now part of Allen's entourage. He snorted, leading to their enthusiastic explanation of his designation as VIP, originated by Heidi and gleefully maintained to fluster him. He rolled his eyes, resulting in giggles.

He and Erin exchanged a look. She read his mind and nodded. He told their new brother and sisters in Christ they were enjoying getting to know them, then asked if they would like to join them for dinner tonight. They laughed when Erin promised it wouldn't just be sandwiches again.

Gui admitted soberly he wasn't ready to be alone just yet, so he was happy to accept. Reina was up for it, too. Teresa thought it over as Alissa called to obtain permission from her parents, saying she had made friends among the wedding party. When Teresa committed to the plan and Alissa's parents learned she would still be with their daughter, they gave their consent.

A restaurant was selected where they would meet, then everyone left to go home and change. Gui would follow his mom home to drop off the sign she prized, then they'd ride together to the meeting point. It turned out she was uncomfortable driving at night.

Erin surprised Allen, following him to their room. His attempt to change clothes took longer than expected, because of it! He was caught pleasantly off-guard. When he asked what she was doing, he was told she was taking his virginity, again!

"Me and my big mouth," he muttered as she laughed. For the record, he was *not* complaining – *that* would be crazy. He was goofy, not crazy … well, except about her.

CHAPTER 5

Eventually succeeding in getting dressed, they left for the rendezvous, having worked up an appetite. Sandwiches only satisfy to a certain extent, after all. Arriving twenty minutes early, they noticed Gui and Reina drive up as they reached the door and waited for them.

Catching up to them, Gui spoke. "Oh, good! I was hoping to speak to you privately; well, without everyone else around. I've been talking with Mom, and you obviously trust Erin, so she's okay. Allen, I've been gay for years, but now the thought of getting with another guy makes me feel sick! What's happening to me?"

Reina told them, "I don't know how to explain it, so I decided to wait for you. I've just been a sounding board, as much as I can. I'm sympathetic to my son, but there are limits to how much I can stand to hear, if that makes sense. I'm doing my best."

Erin stepped over to put an arm around her. Allen nodded, "It's a heavy load for a mama. I understand."

Turning to Gui, he was blunt. "The others will be

arriving any time, so I'll get right to it. Those same-sex desires never originated with you, Gui. The demons were acting out in you, driving you forward. With them gone, your desires will revert to function according to how God designed you.

"The Spirit of Christ inhabits you now, so your body is His temple. Shameful desires would conflict with the real love you have embraced for the One who delivered you from that bondage. You want to please Him as a new creation in Christ Jesus, so old things, like those lusts, have passed away."

"Does this mean I won't want intimacy anymore? Allen, I don't like being alone!"

"God made Eve for Adam back in the beginning for that reason, stating it was not good for man to be alone. If the Lord recognized Adam's need then, He's aware of your need now. One of His names in the Old Testament is Jehovah Jireh, which means 'God will provide.' Give Him time! In the meanwhile, He has given you new friends and a new family you can trust who will stand by you and share your burden, if you'll let them."

"So you think He'll provide a woman for me? I haven't had any desire for a girl since the ninth grade!"

Allen chuckled, "You're about to be sitting at a table surrounded by them, Gui. Not just any women, either! These ladies are exceptional human beings: caring, compassionate, understanding and self-sacrificing. I challenge you to look beyond their femininity and pay close attention to the *quality* of their character.

"If you do, you will come to admire them and realize this is the kind of person you want to share your life with, especially when that one comes along who accepts you for who you are. Bodies age, sag and wrinkle in time, but a quality partner you can trust, who loves you intently despite your faults … brother, that's a priceless treasure! Trust me, as you begin to appreciate *true* beauty, your body will respond, too."

"If we're bringing in a party of ten, we better let the restaurant know," Erin stated.

"Good point, Genie," he replied, "Lead the way. We're with you."

Gui was thinking over what he said. His mom put her arm around him. "He's right. Good people are not limited to one gender, son, or I'd be a man, wouldn't I?"

That got a grin from him. "True, I guess. My sister-in-law is pretty special, too. Maybe the ladies deserve another look, to see if they appeal to me more than they did before. Let's see how much the Lord has changed me."

It wasn't long until the whole group was sitting around the tables put together for them. Sure enough, Alissa had pressed Teresa to tell her about Allen's brush with death when they were alone. She was in awe! Teresa had emphasized she was repeating what Juanita told her, so the teen wasted no time in questioning them on her arrival

Learning how Heidi was living for Christ in Missouri, caring for Ruth, and integrated into their lives now seemed to blow her mind! She thought they would have a restraining order against her. Laurie noted aloud how much Jesus changes people, sharing her own testimony as an example.

The inspiration continued as Dani and Emily shared theirs, as well. The newcomers were enthralled with all the Lord had done for them, the work of restoration He was still doing. Erin and Allen shared how they got together and she came to Christ, even tying it into the encounter with Heidi and Laurie's testimony. It seemed to have a profound impact on their listeners.

Teresa was amazed. "It's like something from a storybook. No wonder Carlos and my cousin were so moved!"

Allen grasped Erin's hand, nodding toward her. "Forget the old damsel in distress theme. She rescued me and Jesus rescued her!"

"Thank you for sharing that," Gui told them. "It gives me hope. If He went to such lengths to bring the two of you together from totally different worlds, I suppose He must have someone for me." He turned his attention to their girls. "You ladies – wow! That you are willing to put yourselves out there without fear, baring your hearts when the world is so judgmental ... I don't know if I could do that. You challenge me! Allen told me you are exceptional people. I see what he means."

They smiled. Emily said, "Dad's kind of biased, but we're okay with that."

Alissa had a quiet exchange with Denise, sitting beside her. Denise chuckled, "She is curious why you refer to Allen as Dad."

Emily opened her mouth, but Laurie started bouncing in her chair, "Ooo, Ooo, I got this! Emily, can I tell her?" The older woman smiled and laughed, then said to go ahead. "We were born again when he told us about Jesus and we received Him. That makes him our father in the faith! For me and Em, who never had a loving father, it means the world to us! It's the same with Heidi, too."

The teen tried to absorb her words. "Heidi? The woman who tried to *kill* Allen thinks of him as her Dad now?"

Erin weighed in, "It's hard to believe, isn't it? Jesus changes *everything*. The old Heidi enslaved to a demon is long gone. The new Heidi who loves Jesus has taken her place! She has volunteered to put her life on the line since then, sweetie. She's 6 feet 3 inches, but the biggest thing about her is her heart!"

Allen spoke up, "Alissa, we took her with us to Missouri because her former coven, led by her mother, wants her dead." *That* shocked the new believers more than anything they had heard so far. "When she failed to kill me, they turned on her."

Reina looked sick, "Her own mother?"

"Love is outside their capabilities, Reina. They have sold themselves to do evil, so nothing good comes from them. This family the Lord has put together, led by Him, is all she has in the world now. She lives isolated from all that was familiar to her before, for her own safety. You said your newfound faith will isolate you, too, Alissa. Would it be okay if I ask Heidi to call you? You could hear what Jesus did for her, directly from her own mouth. I was thinking it might make you both feel a little less isolated."

She took a deep breath, "Y-yeah. If you trust her with your mom, she must be okay now. I'd like that, I think."

Teresa wrapped an arm around her shoulders and gave her a proud squeeze. "My prize pupil is turning out to be quite a lady, don't you think?" The teen grinned as all agreed!

They visited for a long while and tipped the wait staff generously. When Reina was ready to go home, she departed with Gui after hugs were exchanged. Teresa also had to get Alissa home, so they reluctantly bid the group farewell. This left the couple with the three musketeers, plus Denise.

They discussed what to do next. Allen was tired and wanted to go rest, but the younger folks were wound up. Erin wasn't as tired as he was, but became enthusiastic about returning to the house when he offered her a foot rub. The girls laughed at his bribe. He just shrugged and gave them a cheesy grin.

Erin told them, "You don't understand how much I love having my feet rubbed. Truthfully, I think I get just as much pleasure from watching *him* do it. For him, it's an act of love, and it shows!"

The ladies decided to continue with their night out, while the elder couple returned to the house. It had been a long fruitful day. Allen was grateful for the breather. Erin oohed and aahed as he kept his word to her, then they cuddled in bed. He was out in no time!

CHAPTER 6

When he woke the next morning, he opened his eyes to find himself looking into hers. Grinning, they said good morning. Her hand was lazily rubbing up and down his forearm, ruffling the hairs.

"Feel better?" she asked.

"Uh-huh," he replied, his hand going to her side, then following it down to the curve of her hip, "Feeling *real* good, now."

She chuckled, propping her head up on her elbow. "I was kind of worried. It's not like you to fizzle out ahead of everyone else, especially when you know our time here is so limited. I know how much you love being a part of their lives."

He nodded, "I do. They mean a lot to me, our girls in particular. When the Lord uses me to help others, though, it's like I have a purpose for living!"

She smiled and kissed his forehead, "I see that, every time. What do you think drained you so much yesterday, love?" Grinning, she added quickly, "And don't you blame it on my taking your 'virginity'!" He burst out laughing. "Yeah, I know how you think. Don't even try going there!"

He couldn't help admiring her, "How do you do that, wake up with perfect hair?"

"Do you know what time it is?" she answered his question with another. He shook his head no, not ready to look away from her yet. "It's 9:30. You've slept eleven hours, dear. I've been up for a while, worked out, showered, and done my hair. I laid back down and watched you sleep until I decided you had enough, then started running my hand over you. What caused you to become so exhausted?"

He thought for a moment, "Nerves, I guess, Genie. Like your mini golf the other night revealed how you had overtaxed yourself, my body relaxed after how intently I focused on getting the wedding right."

She grimaced, "You handled it so perfectly – well, except for that 'oops' moment – I wouldn't have guessed it was such a strain on you."

He confided, "I've never done anything like that before, Erin. I wanted to get it right, not mess up the memory for those two. It felt like I was under a microscope. The last thing I wanted was to foul up whatever the Lord might bring about, during or after the ceremony. I was trying too hard! The Lord had it all in hand, even the 'oops'. I'm pretty sure that happened for Laurie, to show her it's okay to mess up sometimes."

She looked thoughtful. "I also knew I was going to have to confront Guillermo about his demon. That had me keyed up, too. I didn't want to offend or alienate him, which could have happened *so easily*. God worked it out. I shouldn't have worried, but I guess I couldn't help it."

"You worrywart!" she teased. He grinned. "I was so proud of you, absolutely amazed at how you handled all of it! If you had mishandled Gui, it wouldn't have been him to cause you trouble, it would have been Reina. That's one very protective mother! The Lord guided you yet again. Gui's deliverance resulted in salvation for all four there. God trusts you, dear heart! Why don't you?"

He looked down. "Because I've made mistakes, Erin. I'm afraid I'll make more."

"Yes, you will. It's called being human," she spoke softly, "yet the Lord trusts you to be faithful. He directs you, and He *doesn't* make mistakes. Surely you don't think the ones you make will catch Him by surprise? You just said you thought your 'oops' moment served a purpose for the girl that practically idolizes you."

He looked up at the unexpected insight. "You certainly didn't plan to stammer, but God incorporated your misstep into His plan before it ever happened! Don't be afraid of making a mistake, love. Look forward to them, to see how God displays His sovereignty in working them out for good!"

He wrapped her up in his arms and held her tight. "I love you so much! I had a moment after the ceremony when I felt so exposed, expecting all those people to confront me, demanding to know who I think I am to perform a wedding – and then *you* were there. You held me, said I did good, and everything was all right after that.

"It wasn't just you, either. I thought I was obligated to greet the guests, but Carlos ran interference. Even when Juanita's mom was displeased, her dad handled it, so I was shielded. The Lord has dealt so kindly with me! With His protection and your support, I'm doing things that are *way* over my head. Thank you!"

She replied, "I love that you appreciate me, Allen, but thanks aren't necessary. You know what you mean to me. I'm just guarding my heart!"

"In other words, me," he filled in.

"Uh-huh. Isn't that what I said?" she grinned.

After they got up and around, she linked them together for their Bible study/fellowship. Heidi was introduced to the newest believers and they to her. She was so excited at the news it cracked them up.

Andrew said Delilah was unhappy with him, but wouldn't tell him why. Ever insightful, Danielle suggested perhaps his turning to Christ wasn't welcome news to her. Impressive, Allen thought, since they hadn't shared what Al predicted before he passed. He and Erin said nothing, not wanting to make it a self-fulfilling prophecy, but promised to listen whenever he needed to talk. The whole group prayed for them.

With so many on the line, they made prayer and the study of scripture priorities, then enjoyed fellowship, when paying attention wasn't so vital. The words of brethren are not unimportant, but the word of God carries life. The respectful silence during the study made it clear they agreed. The discussion that followed indicated it wasn't falling on deaf ears.

Someone made mention of the Catholic Bible. Allen suggested procuring a King James Version or a derivative. He expounded, "Primarily, I use the New King James Version, referencing others at times for clarity as the Spirit leads. The Catholic version is suspect, due to being subjected to the slanted viewpoint of the Vatican who claims preeminence over it. God's Word is perfect, but clergy are only human!

"It also embraces documents that do not pass muster as inspired by God, such as the Apocrypha. When our faith stands *entirely* on the inerrancy of scripture, rather than the teachings of clergy, that scripture *must be* above recrimination. A book containing errors leads people into error.

"Who decides what is true and what is error? The answer is Jesus Himself! For anyone else, it would be guesswork. Faith cannot stand on that! Without submitting one's self to Christ, even the Bible can be misunderstood, misapplied and misused to support erroneous doctrines.

"That's why the Lord doesn't clam up and let the Bible do all His talking for Him. Without the Shepherd, the sheep will stray and become prey. He knows we need Him, so He remains close to us, closer than a brother. He opens the scriptures to us on request, so endorsing which writings belong to Him! This teaching is a function of the Holy Spirit."

Allen intended to broach the subject of Holy Spirit baptism with Andrew privately later, but Emily enthusiastically asked if he had received it. She had been so impacted by her baptism in the Spirit that she wanted to share the experience with everyone. He couldn't blame her. Andrew was curious, so he described how He operates to strengthen the believer, explaining and reminding him of scripture, sustaining all who receive Him until we see Jesus.

He wasn't ready to speak in other tongues. It seemed over the top to him. Allen told him the Lord would hear his request and grant the gift when he was ready. Erin related her hesitance at first, then her envy when Heidi received it ahead of her. He listened closely. She had earned his respect in a big way. She chuckled as she warned him that when he did decide to receive God's gift, he'd kick himself for waiting!

Allen kidded Carlos by asking if marriage was worth the wait. His response was a resounding "Yes, sir!" It got everyone laughing. He declared, "It's different now, better than it was; almost like we were holding back, before. She is *so hot*!" Juanita giggled.

Reina cut in, "Hey, hey! Don't forget your mother's on the line, too. I'm glad you're happy, but there's only so much I want to hear! Do I need to hang up?"

That brought more laughter all around as the newlyweds assured her that wasn't necessary, they'd stop. Guillermo was so cracked up he couldn't rein it in after that, which kept the rest laughing, too. They gave up trying to talk. Erin said she'd text everyone the plans when they were decided, then they hung up.

The two of them chuckled for some time. "He's right, you know," Erin told Allen. "There's a freedom with you I never experienced in sex before we met. People say that piece of paper doesn't mean anything, but the commitment we share means something to *me*. I relax with you, secure in the knowledge you'll still be with me when the fun is over. Putting our commitment in writing has meant more to me than I ever thought it would."

"I have nothing to compare it to, since I've never had sex outside of marriage," he replied. "It's a good thing, too, I suppose. I don't know how to hold anything back. If I had given my heart away in a one-night stand, I think it would have about killed me. I'm not wired to handle that! Mom told me once that even when my first marriage went sour, it still provided a measure of protection for me. I guess that's what she meant."

She took him in her arms, kissed him, then looked him in the eye, "My tender-hearted man! You *are* my heart, yet you've given yours to me. Don't worry, I will always take good care of it!"

Smiling, he kissed her back. "I have no doubt of that. I trust you, with everything in me. I'm in good hands!"

She shivered in his embrace, then giggled. "We need to come up with a plan, so I can text it out. If we keep talking like this, I won't be able to keep my "good hands" to myself! You know where that will lead. You can trust me on *that*, too."

He laughed, gave her a quick kiss, and stepped back as they released each other, "Oh, I do − not that I'd mind, though."

She grinned, "Later, Sweet Talker, definitely! Right now, let's feed my diabetic, so he's up for activities later."

CHAPTER 7

"Activities" turned out to be different from what he was expecting when she used the term. She got them together for lunch and informed everyone where they were going, citing a name that meant nothing to him. Everyone else was happy about it. He asked what it was, but she said it was a surprise and he'd have to wait and see.

That was all it took for her to co-opt everyone's assistance in keeping him in the dark! It amused their girls when he tried to schmooze them into telling him about their destination, but they wouldn't budge. They just said it would be fun.

They had their three girls, the waitresses, the newlyweds, and the four who received Christ the day before. Since Erin and Allen planned to go home the next day, they wanted to hang out with them while they could. The surprise ended up being a fun park enclosed in giant hangar-type buildings.

The main attraction was a set of enclosures where a person could float above a tremendously powerful fan, like those seen on TV! There were climbing walls almost to the ceiling. Climbers wore safety harnesses to prevent falls and lower them to the ground when they reached the top.

An obstacle course was elevated above a man-made river that circulated to sweep the hapless (wearing life jackets, of course) over a small waterfall into a waiting lagoon, aptly called 'The Tears of the Fallen.' Whoever completed the course without falling could climb a pedestal to ride the 'Zipline of Glory.' It would carry the champion on a victory lap across the hangar, then outside to the other hangar, where it ended at the opposite end of that building!

He'd never seen anything like the place! There was a shop that sold athletic wear for those who came unprepared, from basic swimwear to famous name brands. Laser tag was available, with video games and table games like air hockey and billiards.

They had a blast! He was stoked for the floating chambers, having always been curious. It felt like flying, something he had dreamed about since childhood. Reina was hilarious to watch! She called it the adventure of a lifetime, afterward. His girls and Juanita kept trying to get him to climb the wall. He refused, along with Reina and Denise, who was nervous about falling.

Emily made it to the top! Dani came within two or three feet before she lost her grip. The wall was 36 feet tall, stacked as three 12-foot sections. Only Carlos came close to matching Dani's height before losing it. Erin was game but lost her grip halfway up. Laurie and Alissa started side by side, but Laurie's limited reach worked against her. Ten feet up, she lunged for a handhold and missed. She came down laughing. Alissa made another four feet before losing it, too.

Teresa approached Denise and Allen, encouraging them to give it a try. Gui overheard and joined in, telling them that the two of them would go last. Laurie told them they couldn't do any worse than she did; besides, the safety harness would keep them from falling. They shrugged at each other, then he said he'd try, if she would. Fran cheered when her friend agreed. The younger girl had just started into the second section, when she dropped off with a scream, followed by laughter!

Allen took his time, and was reaching for the third section when he slipped loose. No one was more surprised than he was at the height he attained! Gui attacked the wall recklessly, losing his footing a mere four feet off the ground, laughing hard. Teresa got halfway up before falling at the same point Erin did. Fran backed out, claiming a fear of heights. Gui heckled Juanita as she started, getting her giggling so that she couldn't even get going. She promised he'd pay for that!

A few tried the obstacle course (Laurie, Juanita, Carlos, and Alissa), only to end up in the water. It was very entertaining to watch, though! The group ended up having their own air hockey tournament, which got pretty competitive. Teresa won it, but it was very hard fought. Fran's quick reflexes were nearly a match for her.

Once Gui's concentration was locked in, Juanita bided her time until she saw her chance. Sneaking in behind him, she grabbed his ribs with her fingertips! He was never able to focus after that, his nerves thoroughly rattled. "Payback!" she crowed, quite satisfied. Allen always considered himself pretty good at the game, but not against these folks! It was still a lot of fun, though.

He thanked Erin for bringing them there as they were leaving, which was seconded several times. She declared they'd be back since he got higher on the wall than she did! He returned her grin, marveling at her competitiveness. His longer reach gave him an advantage, he mused aloud. She acknowledged the possibility, but was sure she could do better. After all, Emily and Dani did good, and they weren't much taller than her. Laurie ventured that she'd like to see Heidi try. They agreed she had the build for it.

They decided on seafood for dinner. Alissa's parents consented to let her go, but said they were jealous! Invited to join the party, they declined, thanking them for the offer, but they were about to eat dinner at home. The time together with everyone was precious, so Erin and Allen lingered, reluctant to say goodbye. They reminded the new believers they'd be in touch via the daily conference calls, though travel the next day would pre-empt that one.

When Teresa and Alissa were preparing to leave, he surprised the teen with a small Bible he had picked up when replacing the one he gave to Emily. She was very pleased, especially when she found it would fit in her purse. He and Erin each got a big hug and thank you for the gift.

Moved, Teresa asked about it. Allen explained that with non-believing parents, he thought she might have trouble obtaining one of her own. She replied his concern was justified and the gift was inspired. Just another case of the Lord knowing what would be needed, he pointed out! They'd also be praying for her family to receive Christ.

Denise cracked up when he told her it was fun being driven up the wall with her today! Erin put Fran on the spot when she inquired how the date the night before had gone, in front of everyone. The waitress blushed and said it went okay, but refused to dish details when the girls pressed for them. She did say the new peace the Holy Spirit supplied kept fear out of it.

Erin told her they were satisfied to praise God for that and wouldn't need more information. She was looking pointedly at their girls when she said it, which drew looks of disappointment from Laurie and Emily; however, all three heartily agreed when she added the main thing was knowing Fran was okay. Their concern touched her. She thanked them for caring.

Allen spoke up, "Carlos and Juanita, Reina, Gui, and Teresa: do you know how *inspiring* it is to see a family give their hearts to Jesus?" They grinned as the rest applauded. "You know He's gonna use your testimony to bring in more, don't you?"

Heads nodded in agreement. Carlos declared, "Mr. Allen, you're right, but we want you to know something. *This family sitting right here around this table means the world to us!* We're blood, too, joined by the blood of the One who died for us. We love you all, am I right?" he looked at the others, who nodded emphatically. He finished with a grin, "Because of that, you'll never be rid of us, you know? You're all part of our Mexican family now, even if you don't speak Spanish or have brown skin."

It got them all laughing. "You have a point," Allen replied, "and the Head of our family is a Jew. Who understands the importance of family better than Jews and Hispanics?"

"Nobody!" Carlos asserted, his grin broadening.

Gui put an arm around his shoulders, "That's right, bro."

Allen quipped, "Suddenly I have a craving for tacos! See what you did?" It must've hit Reina's funny bone. She laughed so hard it turned to tears, which cracked them up even more. They parted on that festive note.

The next morning, the couple flew home after tearful goodbyes with their girls. Stef was stoic but gave both big hugs before they left. Pam made a point of seeing them off, saying she'd be in touch. Allen had an impression something was on her mind. While talking at the airport, Erin said she had the same feeling. Maybe they could get her and Win on the line after they settled in at home.

It was so nice to get back! Heidi was at work when they arrived. Erin texted her and Anthony to let them know they were home, safe. The travelers promised to stay up until she got off work, so they could see her. Visiting with Ruth, they caught her up on everything that happened. Hearing all the Lord had done gave her cause to rejoice!

Ruth went to bed after dinner, so Erin called Pam. The timing was good. She and Win were together, so the four could visit via speakerphone. Pam was surprised and pleased to hear from them. They told her of their impression that something was on their minds, having noticed they seemed hesitant when they left after the wedding.

Win owned it, "That's on me. Something happened that's been bothering both of us. Pam told me how she came into possession of the Bible we're reading, how she nearly lost it, and the odd way it came back to her. She said you explained all that weirdness, Allen, so it made sense. The *thought* that an angel in disguise brought it back stretches our imagination, but nothing else makes sense! She thought, well, we both hoped you might have some insight to help us now."

Allen exchanged a look with Erin. "I'll do my best, Win. What happened? Are you two okay?"

Pam chimed in quickly, "Oh, yeah, guys, we're fine. It's nothing like that. The night before the wedding, Win had a dream. It seemed very real to him. When he told me about it, I found it disturbing and I haven't been able to shake that feeling. I wondered if you might have some wisdom to bring to the table. Your 'entourage' was talking today about your dream the same night, how it kept the wedding from being swarmed by bees. Now I'm wondering if Win's dream came from God. Tell them what you saw, Win."

"I saw the house, your house, Erin, like I was looking down on it from above. As I watched, it was like a sinkhole opened beneath it. The whole building fell in; nothing was left but a hole that seemed bottomless! I didn't see anyone, but I *knew* the house wasn't empty, though I couldn't tell who was in it. I was shocked and grieved at the loss of life that took place with the disaster. That's all I saw. It seemed so real! I've felt like a horse kicked me in the ribs ever since, like I *really* watched someone die. I can't shake the feeling! Am I losing my mind?"

"If he is, it's contagious," Pam declared, "'cause ever

since he told me about it, I've felt unsettled, like it's a premonition or something." Erin had seized his hand; it bothered her, too.

"It's something, for sure. You're not crazy, at least no more than I am. Genesis records how the Pharaoh of Egypt had a dream that bothered him, too. When his advisors couldn't interpret its meaning, his butler remembered having a dream in prison and how a fellow prisoner explained it. Pharaoh sent for Joseph to be brought up from the prison, who interpreted the dream's warning. A famine was coming that would have decimated the world population, but Joseph found favor with Pharaoh and wisely prepared for it. Those events *created* the Egyptian empire of ancient times."

He heard 'whoa' and a gasp. "Just a moment," he requested, then bowed his head to ask the Lord about it, Erin's hand still in his. It didn't take more than a moment.

"Okay, this is what I believe God showed me. Because you are calling on Him to show you He is real, He is revealing a future event that will directly affect you. It is just for you two, okay? If you tell others, they *will* think you're crazy. Pam, A*C*E is not your future. It may not be swallowed up in a sinkhole, but it's not going to last. If you don't have a fallback plan for your livelihood, you need to make one, because the company's days are numbered.

"I'm not telling you this to scare you, just to warn you, which is the purpose of the dream. Because it came from God, you will find peace in this knowledge, rather than fear. Your Maker has your best interests in mind!"

CHAPTER 8

Pam heaved a sigh, then asked, "Erin, if that's true, it's *your* business going down the tubes. Doesn't that scare you to death?"

"It did, Pam, the first time I heard it, but this isn't the first time. God's been showing us things that line up with Win's dream, though not as dramatic. He's preparing me, the same as you. It's coming, but not immediately, and the indications are that I won't lose everything – I'll be okay. Would you be, without this job?"

"Well, I think I could freelance, with my experience," Pam replied, "but I'm not sure I would do it. I have enough put back so I wouldn't be desperate, but I'd have to go back to work eventually. With maybe a little schooling, I have bankable skills, once I decide which to develop. I'll be okay, too. I haven't committed to a specific fallback career yet, I've just been building a cushion toward the day when I'll have to choose, aware it was coming. Most of us don't put off retirement as long as you did."

Erin chuckled, "Most people have something to look

forward to in retirement. I didn't, until Allen came along. I'm not alone, now, and Christ has built a family around us like I never dreamed of having!"

"I don't understand, Allen," Win mused, "Why did this dream come to me if it's about Pam's future? Shouldn't it have been hers, instead?" Allen laughed, while Erin grinned. He wished he could see Pam's face at the moment, since she said nothing.

"Why do you think, my friend? It must affect you, too, don't you think? Would you have any connection to that house, if not for her? This dream would seem to indicate that you're not just dating. Your lives are entwined, Doc.

"God would not have sent you the dream, if it didn't affect you. It did, though. You said it *really* bothered you. That's because you care about her, maybe more than you were willing to admit. And if you think that exposes *your* feelings too much, I'll ask just one more question. Why hasn't *she* asked the question you just asked?"

"...uh..." Pam was completely silent. "Oh... my... God!" the light dawned on him. "You believe your future... isn't separate from me!" he exclaimed. "You're *okay* with that?"

"I know what I want, Win, and I'm still here with you. I believe in *you*. Is the idea of a future with me okay with you?" she shot back.

"Okay? Are you kidding? Pam, *I love you!* I've just been afraid to say so, 'cause I thought it might scare you away!"

She chuckled, "Nope, still here. You don't scare me at all, and you never will."

"Win!" Allen raised his voice to get his attention.

"Yes, sir?" he replied.

"We're gonna hang up now, before we start feeling like we're intruding on a private conversation." Erin cracked up laughing. He heard Pam giggle for the first time. "One last thing I want to point out, though; nothing you said so far qualifies as a proposal, so don't get it in your head that she said yes, understand?"

Erin about fell out of her chair laughing, but managed agreement, "That's true, Win!"

He didn't reply, so they said goodbye and hung up. It kept them chuckling until Heidi got home. Their red-headed Amazon wrapped her arms around the both of them and crushed them to her in delight. "I sure missed you two!" she gushed. "Miss Ruth slept a lot while you were gone. I got lonesome!" They visited for a while, then invited her to crash on the couch if she wanted. She said she would sleep better in her own bed. By that time, he and Erin were more than ready to do the same.

The next day, Erin put in a call to the former customer that was on staff as a coach at a prestigious university. He was shocked and pleased to hear from her. He hadn't returned to A*C*E since starting a family. That kind of thing didn't fit with family life, but his memories of Erin were pleasant.

She chuckled, "You apparently don't remember the pain I put you through!"

"Oh, yes, I do," he said, "but you made it fun."

He asked what led to her call. She explained the odd situation concerning Laurie and how she left gymnastics after difficulties at home caused her to leave it, too. The young lady adopted Erin and Allen as parents, and now she had agreed to put on a one-time exhibition of her skills for her new family. She needed proper facilities to do so, with access to those facilities for a few weeks to shake off nearly six years' worth of rust.

The man asked her name. When Erin gave it to him, he let out a low whistle, "Laurie Parcille! Are you kidding me? Erin, I scouted her several years ago. We had high hopes of getting her into our program, but then she just disappeared. Her mother refused to tell us anything. If that young lady wants to use our gym, *I'll* make sure she can. Have her call me, okay?" He told Erin not to worry about costs. He'd let her know if any came up he couldn't waive.

She then called Laurie to update her. She promised she'd call. She laughed when Erin warned her the coach might still try to recruit her, and would almost certainly be watching her practice.

"Let him watch!" she said. "It'll help me bring my 'A' game." Allen admired her 'go get "em" attitude and told her so, which got a giggle. "I'm not gonna enroll, no matter what he offers. He can't offer you guys, and I want to be with you!" she declared. "Besides, I have no desire to pursue gymnastics after this."

He wondered aloud if she had thought about teaching it, once she joined them. It gave her pause. She said she hadn't considered it, but it might be worth thinking about. A girl still has to make a living!

He and Erin began looking at houses with six or more bedrooms. Certain facts became clear as they did. Renting wasn't really an option for a house that size. They'd have to buy or build. They needed free access for Ruth, which meant either a single-floor plan or an elevator for multiple floors. She had a motorized wheelchair she didn't use much, but it would be a necessity in a bigger house, a fact she willingly acknowledged. Last, they needed parking for at least six vehicles.

It seemed building would be the way to go. Over three weeks' time, they found nothing that satisfied all these specifications. They became weary of looking. Praying once more, they began to look for properties suitable to build what they wanted.

In the process, Erin found a house and property half a mile outside the city limits. The price was $3.5 million, the same as she paid for the house in California! Allen considered it too costly, but the more Erin looked at the pictures and description, the more it tweaked her interest. It had 8 bedrooms, 7 and a half baths, an indoor pool, two 3-car garages with paved parking for 6 more cars, and an easy access design throughout. She wanted to go look at it, so they did. She convinced Ruth and Heidi to go along.

Built on a rise, situated on three acres, it had plenty of trees to keep it cool. It was all on one floor, except for an observatory built over the centrally located living room, beneath which was a basement den. The floors were connected by an elevator. It was everything they wanted! Allen's heart sank.

The kitchen sat behind the living area, adjoining the dining room, where sliding glass doors provided entry to the enclosed pool. That boasted duplicate enclosed showers with facilities attached. Two wide hallways spurred off to each side of the living room, centrally navigating both wings of the house, passing two bedrooms on either side to end in doors that accessed a garage. In the left wing, two bathrooms separated the front and back bedrooms, accessible from adjoining bedrooms and the hall.

The right-wing was larger. The first two bedrooms on either side were dual masters with a built-in bathroom in each. The front bedrooms were separated by another bathroom, while the back bedrooms were separated by the laundry room. The final half bath was located in the basement den. Skylights throughout kept the place bright and cheery. It was perfect, except for the price – and it wasn't overpriced, not at all.

They finished their tour, then returned to the van. The ladies were excited, but it didn't take long for them to notice his silence.

Erin inquired, "What's wrong, love?"

"Erin, we can't afford that. *You* can't afford that. Your company would collapse if you liquidated your assets to pay for it! Financing it would lock us into payments taxing even the income you are providing. I love it, too, but how would we manage it?"

"We would struggle to make it work, Sweet Talker, if it were just us trying to do it," she reassured him, "but we're not alone, remember? Let's pray and ask God for what we want, right now, together, okay? Surely you don't believe the price is too much for Him?"

"Of course not, Genie. But until you came into my life, money was always a struggle for me," Allen confessed. "I don't have much experience with Him providing large-scale finances, none, in fact. I've always known He *can* do it, but He's never saw fit to do it for me. Maybe He will for you, though. I guess it doesn't hurt to ask."

She took his chin in her hand and looked deep into his eyes, "He will do it for *us*, my love, not just for me, because it pleases Him and suits His purpose. He prepared you to minister over your lifetime, but until you received His miracle, surviving the Devil's attempt on your life, you didn't get to do it, did you? Ministry opened up to you at the time the Lord appointed for it."

"You felt forgotten by Him until then, but now you are surrounded by people who love you because you were obedient when the time came. We're shopping for a house to shelter those He has brought to us because they need our love and care. Don't you know He'll finish what He started? He's the Good Shepherd, and we're caring for His lambs. We're not alone in this!"

Ruth was in tears, knowing exactly where he was coming from, but recognizing the Lord's wisdom his partner spoke. They prayed then, putting their petition before Him. He brought His supernatural peace that passes all understanding. When they finished, Erin looked at Mom and Heidi. Each nodded, then she looked at him. He shrugged and inclined his head, feeling completely out of his depth.

She smiled reassuringly, "It'll be okay, love, wait and see. I need to go back in there to put down a deposit, as an act of faith. Will you come stand in faith with me?"

He thrust fear aside, determined to be there for her as she had so faithfully stood with him, and nodded. The pair walked back in and he held her hand in silence as she negotiated a non-refundable deposit of twenty thousand dollars to hold the property while she made payment arrangements. He hoped his fear wouldn't cancel out her faith!

They returned to the van, where she had them join hands. With an ear-to-ear grin, she said, "Agree with me. It's *ours!*" They all did, in Jesus' name.

CHAPTER 9

The next day, they went to the bank to discuss financing. He didn't say much. Truthfully, he was impressed they were taken seriously. Arrangements were made to have the property appraised and they promised they would be in touch. When Erin set up their conference call fellowship, she broke the news of what they were doing.

Laurie broke down bawling, followed by Emily and Heidi. It sounded like everyone was crying! They could not believe the family was making room for them to live together. Though Heidi was already in on it, she couldn't keep it together, either. Allen finally realized how this plan was of the Lord, an example of how He accepts all who trust in Him. If He chose to use them in this way, He would not fail to provide their sufficiency.

Ruth came out of her room to all the tears and wanted to know what was wrong. They told her they had informed everyone about the house and the plans to make room for them, which brought tears to her eyes.

She sat down, and after a moment managed a laugh,

"Will you all *stop*? Please!" Some giggles punctuated the sniffles.

"Sorry, Grandma," Laurie choked out, "it's just – to be wanted and welcomed – means so much! Are you okay with this, too?"

"Honey, I'm thrilled! I'm looking forward to meeting all of you and getting to know you. Whoever won't be moving here, I hope you'll still come to see us. It looks like we'll have plenty of room to put you up," she laughed. "I can't do much, but I can still manage hugs, and I've got one for all of you!"

"She's really good at it, too!" Heidi announced proudly, which got more giggles and a grin from Ruth.

"How many bedrooms will you have available?" Dani asked practically.

"Six," Erin replied, "all good size, too. We can double up if it comes to it, but I don't think it will be necessary. Laurie and Emily made their intentions clear, and Heidi is with us. Dani, there's room for you, if you're interested. Is anyone else thinking of coming, long-term?"

Carlos spoke up, "Our lives are here, Erin, along with our families. We hope to lead more of them to Christ."

Juanita quickly added, "We'll come to visit, though."

"That's what I'm thinking, too," Gui chimed in.

Fran was thoughtful, "It sounds like space won't be a problem for you. I don't plan to move, but things change, so you never know. Don't worry about saving room for me. If I do move, I'd probably want my own place. I'm used to that, you know?"

"Totally understandable," Erin agreed. "I was planning to set up temporary quarters for visitors or anyone who needs a place to flop while searching for a place of their own. Sharing a big house doesn't appeal to everyone; I get that. Sounds like three, maybe four rooms out of six are spoken for, at the moment. That leaves two to play with, also a den, as well. If anyone has a change of heart, talk to us, okay? God is giving us this space for a reason."

Dani was still thinking, "Erin, those of us who take up your offer, you'll let us help pay our way, won't you? I don't think any of us wants to live off you, free of charge. That wouldn't be right."

Erin chuckled, "Since when did I become a sucker?" Giggles could be heard again. "No, ma'am, tenants will pay rent! However, since you are family, the amount will depend on your income, and what you can afford. Eviction isn't something you need to fear, but if you cross me, I might just wring your neck!"

"Yep, that's Mom," Laurie confirmed with a chuckle, "Some things never change."

Emily spoke quietly, "I can't wait to go home!"

The call ended with a prayer and thanksgiving for the Lord's provision. It bothered Allen that Andrew hadn't responded, but Erin reminded him his paramedic duties could explain why he didn't. Not everyone answered every call, but if Al was right about his niece, Allen worried about Andrew getting hurt. The big man had a tender heart, and Al had said Delilah wasn't trustworthy. He kept him in his prayers.

The next day, the bank called. The property appraised well over the asking price, at almost $3.9 million. If the couple would put $1.6 million down, payments would be approximately $12,300 per month for a 30-year mortgage. Erin asked calmly if there would be any penalties for paying it off early. They said no. She promised to call back after they conferred.

He just listened, too rattled to do anything else, as she told him she could raise the down payment, barely. The payments would take up their monthly income, but for the first few years, they'd get most of it back at tax time by writing off the interest. They could live off what was already in the bank in the meanwhile, over $150,000.

It is doable, she insisted, reminding him that the rent

they already pay plus whatever the girls' supply would trim down that excess $2,300 to fit their $10,000 monthly income. She wanted to sign the loan but emphasized it was God who would supply the funding because He ordained what they were doing. Though the numbers boggled him, he knew she was right.

They prayed and he gave his consent, which she wanted more than needed. Overwhelmed, he abandoned himself to trust her judgment and the Lord's faithfulness; he told both of them so. She assured him he wouldn't regret it, kissed him, then called her accountant to arrange the down payment.

That afternoon, Allen napped in his recliner. He saw the note the bank had prepared, several pages thick, the term '30 years' in bold print nearly jumping off the page. As he beheld it, the term was struck through and *replaced with '6 months'*. A huge stamp came down on the form, marking it "Paid in full!" Another paper was laid atop it, a handwritten note. It read, *"Because like Me, thou art the helper of the fatherless."* Psalms 10:14 was referenced.

He woke, bailed out of the chair and practically ran for his Bible. Erin saw his haste and thought he was headed for the bathroom. When he let out an excited whoop, she rushed to the bedroom. The scripture read, in the old King James:

"Thou hast seen it; for thou beholdest mischief and spite, to requite it with thy hand: the poor committeth himself unto thee; thou art the helper of the fatherless."

He sat on the bed and cried, thanking God as Erin sat beside him, her arm around his shoulders. Telling her of his vision, it wasn't long before she was in tears, too. The Lord had revealed His plan; within six months, the property would be theirs, free and clear. Hallelujah!

They discussed it with Ruth. She was as bowled over as they were. As they talked it out, it became clear what they were doing was opening up a kind of orphanage, a refuge for the abandoned and dispossessed to receive acceptance and healing. Erin was completely overwhelmed at the realization, having been orphaned herself! *No wonder* she was so drawn to this calling, she told them. Even before she understood it, she knew it was something she had to do, because it was right. Now she knew why.

Ruth laughed and laughed, telling them this was *her* mother's dream. Her mom always wanted to open an orphanage, to love and care for kids who did not have that support. The fact their care would be for adults rather than children didn't make it less meaningful. Society provides some support for bereaved kids, but God recognizes the hurting hearts of adults who never received what they so needed, what they still need. It delighted her that *she* would get to do what her mother never found the opportunity to do, even if it was in her twilight years.

As for Allen, he would get to teach them about their heavenly Father and model how He loves them! Such an honor bestowed on him when he considered himself such a failure – there were no words adequate to express his feelings. "He said I'm like Him in this way," he thought to himself! It's what he always wanted, and if God said it, it had to be true. His thought concluded, "Maybe I won't be ashamed when I stand before Jesus, after all, having loved those He loves!"

On Friday, they signed the papers and made the down payment, receiving the keys. They moved in a few days later, after setting up services, turning on utilities, giving notice to their landlord, as well as Heidi's, and packing. Moving is a complex pain, but they were excited enough to offset the stress.

Their tall redhead reminded them of a kid at Christmas, so enthusiastic! They caught Ruth driving her chair from one end of the house to the other, circling the living room back to the kitchen and dining room, looking out at the pool. When asked what she was doing, she declared with a grin she was touring the premises! It was mentioned she was leaving out the observatory and the den, but she shook her head. "I'm headed there next!" she announced, then took off again. As she got on the elevator, she hollered, "Freedom!" It got them laughing.

Over the two weeks after the move, they easily cleaned up the rentals and turned in the keys. Heidi's apartment was under a lease agreement, but management had another tenant lined up, so they didn't cause any trouble. Heidi declared with excitement, "The Lord provided yet again!" Erin set them up with a security system, complete with a remote doorbell response. She said they'd get a break on homeowner's insurance for having it installed, plus Ruth could answer the door from her room if no one else was home. She liked that!

CHAPTER 10

When Heidi called Alissa, they quickly became fast friends. The teen realized the woman who tried to kill Allen was long gone, transformed by the love of Christ into a lady worthy of trust and emulation! It got to where they were talking pretty much every day, but something about it made Allen uncomfortable. He couldn't understand it. He knew Alissa's conversion was real.

When he brought it before the Lord, there was no instant answer. Out and about later, though, a Freemason symbol on a car seemed to jolt him. He called Alissa, surprising her, to ask if her parents were Freemasons. She replied her dad was.

That chilled him. Freemasonry is secretive, for good reason. Riddled with deception among its ranks and having a strong disinformation arm, it holds to a globalist philosophy. Those closest to its heart blatantly worship Satan, though many in it remain unaware. The very few who dared to expose their core beliefs and practices have had to go into hiding, fearing for their lives! Certain Alissa didn't know all this, he thought perhaps it would be best if she didn't know.

Erin was with him, listening on speakerphone. He asked the teen, "Did we tell you Heidi's former coven is looking for her, to kill her?"

"Y-yeah, I remember that. Is she okay?"

"She is, honey, and we're gonna keep her safe, with Jesus' help. He warned us they were looking for her phone number by sneaking around and searching her friends' contacts. Do you have her number listed by name in your contacts?"

"Yeah, Allen, I do. Is that bad? I didn't think anybody in those circles knew about me, or that she's my friend."

"They may not, but we're playing it safe, just in case. We're gonna get her a new phone number. When we do, she'll call and give it to you, 'cause she likes visiting with you."

"I like talking with her, too. She's a good friend, and really smart," she replied.

He chuckled, "We agree, on both points." She giggled. "When you put her new number in your contacts, don't list her name with it. List it as someone else. Erin and I have been telling folks to show it as an alternate number to reach us."

"Hey, that's clever! I'll do that. It wouldn't even show up as a new contact, that way. Thanks! I don't want her to get hurt, especially because of me."

"Us, neither. We love her, and we love you, too. By the way, Erin's here, listening on speaker."

"Hi, Alissa!" Erin spoke up.

"Hi, Erin! I love you guys, too. Thanks for calling!" They said bye, then hung up.

"What do you think, Genie? Does she need a new phone this time, or just to change the number?"

"I think a new number might be enough," she responded, "It's a pain to transfer contacts onto a new phone. You think her dad could be a danger to Heidi?"

"Unknowingly, yes, I do. If he's a rank-and-file Mason, he may not even realize how he's watched. As a parent, it wouldn't surprise me if he checks his kids' phones to keep an eye on them, unaware of the demons looking over his shoulder."

She asked about the Masons, so he told her what he knew. It would be interesting to see if Heidi's knowledge of them was more complete. On arrival home, they told Heidi (who was with Ruth) about Allen's unease, the masonry symbol, and the conversation with Alissa.

She shook her head in frustration, "I never thought about her parents being connected with Freemasonry. You're right. They're not directly hooked in with the coven, but they have their own occult practices powered by the same Devil, who would be happy to pass them information about me. I was being so careful, refraining from texts that could be viewed afterward, but this still got past me!"

Erin put her hand on her arm, "Don't worry about it. You can't live in fear, or you would be *completely* isolated. The Holy Spirit warned Allen, so now you can change your number. Praise the Lord! He's still looking out for you. Plus, you have us keeping watch, a new friend that looks up to you, and through that friendship a support that discourages isolation. Personally, I think you're blessed!"

She grinned, "Me too, now that I think about it. Thank you, I'll change my number right away!" She hugged them and Ruth spread her arms, wanting to be included, which made her giggle.

"I don't want to rush you, Heidi, but the quicker you notify Alissa of your new number, the less she'll worry. She felt bad she might have put you in danger. By the way, I didn't point out her dad might be the risk. I doubt he knows he is, and that would be a heavy load for her to bear."

"Yes, it would," she agreed. "A kid shouldn't carry such

a burden. I won't mention it, either."

Moving back in with Dad and Grandma didn't appeal to Anthony, but he and Louise planned to wade in the pool with the babies, getting them accustomed to the water. When the rest of the ladies arrived, they'd have no lack of help with that! They intended to teach them swimming and water safety later on, but for now just wanted to get them used to it.

Erin, Allen, and Heidi participated, getting the biggest kick out of watching their expressions! It got so they would light up whenever they saw the pool. The four living there concluded maybe it was good they *hadn't* moved in, because crawling babies would keep everyone nervous they might get in and drown. Ruth was very thankful for their decision, though she loved their visits.

Laurie estimated another three to four weeks to be ready for her exhibition. The coach had been encouraging and supportive throughout her practices. He was watchful, stating if she got hurt, he didn't want her to be alone and without help, which made sense. As time went by, more and more people showed interest. It didn't bother Laurie, whose focus was on practice.

This was old hat to her, and her expertise continued to impress onlookers. She gave permission early on that spectators were okay with her. No one had solicited her for enrollment, so far. The only visitors she banned were her coworkers! She told them in no uncertain terms they had to wait to see her routine until her mom and dad were there to watch, too. She was adamant, *no sneak peeks*.

Just let them know the date and time she worked out with the college, the couple told her, and they'd be there. Dani advised them excitement was building in the company ranks over the exhibition, as it had for the wedding. Everyone liked Laurie and had been curious! While some couldn't grasp why she bonded to Allen so intensely, they were pleased he obtained her favor in this matter. He admired how they were so supportive of one another, even those who had not received Christ. If there were any bitterness or unfriendly rivalries among the ladies, he saw no evidence of it.

Stefanie had hired two new wrestlers, according to Emily. Later in conversation with Stef, Erin confirmed it and was told she was in talks with a third young lady. Stef said she had never replaced Heidi, but decided it was high time to fill out the ranks. Business was good; besides, she didn't want to be caught short-handed when 'the three musketeers' moved to Missouri.

Erin chuckled and told her she wasn't sure Dani would be coming. Without batting an eye, Stefanie assured her she would be, trust her. Stef planned to hire two more women for a total of five before she was done.

Noting his lady was quiet after the call, Allen asked what was on her mind. She said Stef was doing what she needed to do. She understood that, but when she was finished, half the staff would be strangers to Erin. The company she founded and invested her life into for decades was moving on without her.

She knew it would with her retirement, but it felt like she was losing something that *mattered* to her. Stef, Dani, and her had been the nucleus at its heart for many years, yet now it looked like Stef would be all that was left of its early days. He mostly listened, but reminded her that indications point to Dani joining them, also pointing out how their bond with her was closer than ever. She was pleased about that, she said, but the change in the company was hard, almost like she was losing her place there.

He put his arms around her. "There's nothing I can do about that, but you will *never* lose your place here with me, if that helps."

"Helps?" she chuckled, "Sweet Talker, I walked away from my place there to be with you." Returning his embrace, she smiled, "That was my house, but this is my *home*," she patted his arms as they held her. "Not a day goes by I don't cherish how wonderful it is to be home with you! Don't mistake my melancholy moments for regret. I don't regret any part of my life with you. Change is sometimes difficult, but with you by my side, I'll get through it. It was time to move on, anyway. A girl can't stay on top of the heap in that world forever."

"Now that's a first, hearing you talk like that," he noted. "You always act like you're invincible, ready, willing and able to prove it, too!"

With a sly grin, she held him closer, "I have you convinced, don't I?" He nodded silently, not sure what was coming next. She deliberately kissed him, with a chuckle.

"My confidence is intact, love, but my ability isn't what it once was. I trust you enough to confide in you. I tire faster than I did when I was younger. I'm not as strong or as fast as I was, either. Experience compensates, some. I've learned to predict my opponent's choices and reduce his options like I'm reading his mind, but outsmarting him isn't the same as overpowering him. I tricked Andrew, remember? I rely on tactics like that to win now, more than I ever did before. Age affects us all, me included."

He shook his head, "I suppose, but you're still more than I can handle."

She laughed heartily and kissed him three times, "Of course I am! I told you I'd always be able to kick your butt, and I meant it! You're slipping as you age, too, so I'll maintain my edge on you. Also, the idea of hurting me repels you and prevents you from going all out against me, therefore you can't win. That's not bravado, just the simple truth!

"You said it, you're defenseless when it comes to me. It's not because I broke through your defenses, but because *you lowered them* to let me close to you. I've been careful *not* to break you down because I love you. That means you can't *lose* anything more than a playful contest from time to time, either, because when I win, you win!"

"That explains why I'm not frightened when you get the best of me," he smiled.

She nodded, "As I always do. I tease you, not to withdraw and frustrate you, but to show my control in choosing to overwhelm you with affection, too. In the end, you don't feel beaten, you feel loved and oh, so wanted ... which is what I had in mind the whole time!"

"Boy, do you have my number," he commented, amazed. Her lips met his, scattering his thoughts. Their eyes locked as she smiled, genuinely pleased.

"I *like* that you know that. I own you, mister, in my own way, which takes nothing away from Christ's claim on both of us. All it means is you're a better man for it, more complete in my embrace. I promise you'll never regret the hold I have on you!"

CHAPTER 11

For nearly two weeks, they had no contact with Andrew. He did not respond to their calls nor join the conference call fellowships. They prayed for him daily. Thirteen days later, he called Allen in the afternoon. His affable 'all is right with the world' cheerfulness quickly proved to be a facade he was unable to hide behind. When asked how he was really doing, he dissembled.

"Allen, Little D is getting harder and harder to understand. Nothing I do seems to keep her happy for long. I give her all my attention and she acts like it's no big deal, but if I start to back off, she gets all lovey-dovey and draws me back in. I don't understand what she wants."

The older man cut him off with a question, point-blank, "Andrew, are you two having sex?"

He hesitated before answering, "Sure, Allen. That's the kind of world we live in. Couples have sex."

"You committed to follow Christ, my brother," he reminded him. "If you stood before Him today, would this matter cause you shame?"

There was a long silence, then an intake of breath, "Yeah, it would. I know it's wrong. When she comes onto me, it's tough to refuse her – but I don't try very hard. It's the only time I feel like I make her happy, but it never lasts very long and it doesn't seem to mean much to her, afterward."

"When we sin, fellowship with Jesus is broken. The peace He brings is forfeited and we lose our perspective, we lose our ability to be objective. She doesn't live for Christ. You know that, don't you?"

"Yeah, she doesn't even want to hear about Him. She turns on the charm to distract me big-time when I mention Him. I really care about her, Allen! I don't want to lose her."

"I understand you're hurting, Andrew. I'm sorry, but truth is the only way to sort this out. *You don't have her, she has you!* She is playing a tug-of-war game with Christ for your heart. You said it yourself, the only time she's happy is when you're sinning with her!

"She doesn't care about you, she just likes pulling your strings to make you jump. You can't have her and Christ both; she won't allow it! Either you decide who you will cleave to, or she will decide for you. If sex is the only time she's happy with you, the two of you won't be a very happy couple, even if you turn your back on the Lord, seems to me."

He chuckled without humor, "For a man who doesn't fight and said every woman in the room could whip him, you're hitting me awfully hard, Allen! I want her to care about me as much as I care about her, but if she doesn't, if you're right, I can't make that happen. I don't want to just break up with her. What if you're wrong about her motives? How can I know?"

"I've only told you the truth, Andrew. I wish it didn't hurt. It comes from Jesus Himself, the source of all truth. You can repent, ask His forgiveness, and be restored in the fellowship with Him you have lost, so He can show you the truth. My guess is if you inform her you are utterly resolved to keep your pants zipped up from now on, she'll have no further use for you. If she's willing to respect your decision and stick beside you, that will prove I was wrong, don't you think?"

"That's a pretty simple test, I guess," he breathed.

"Simple, yes. Easy? No. She won't make it easy for you to stick to your guns. If you do, you may be in for some abuse before she cuts you loose. But at least you'll know where you stand, and know *you* didn't dump *her*."

"That's true. You're a good friend, Allen. I'll take this to the Lord right now."

"I'm here if you need me, Andrew. When you talk to her, I recommend it be in public, with plenty of witnesses, if you know what I mean. We're praying for you."

He thanked Allen and ended the call. Erin heard a bit of the conversation. He filled her in when she asked how the big man was doing.

She shook her head, "Delilah likes to party. It makes her popular with guys, but not the kind that makes a good husband. Honestly, I think she stayed with Andrew as long as she did out of curiosity and because he paid attention to her. If the fun's gone, she will be, too. He can do better." They prayed for him together.

Sure enough, when they went out to dinner that night, she walked out upon hearing of his decision. Repenting to make it right with the Lord after the call, Andrew told Allen he knew it would happen. He was prepared, but it still hurt. The couple listened, not knowing what to say, then prayed with him before he hung up.

Erin was irritated at Delilah's treatment of him. Allen agreed it was shabby, but none of this would have happened if he hadn't dropped his pants for her. Sin can be forgiven, yet consequences still follow. At least she couldn't continue to hurt him, hopefully.

He and Andrew talked often after that, one broken heart relating to another. He couldn't fathom what it must feel like to have a 38-year marriage come to an end. Allen admitted it felt like part of him died until God brought Erin along. Now he understood it was for the best, how Erin's salvation came about largely because he was available to her. She had learned directly from Jesus that it was the only way He could reach her.

Likewise, if Andrew hadn't collided with Delilah in the market that day, he wouldn't have seen and heard the things that led to his receiving God's grace in Christ Jesus as an adult. All these things serve a purpose only He sees ahead of time. We would avoid pain if we could, only to miss out on blessings not yet apparent to our aching hearts.

Their girls heard about the breakup from their coworker, told with a 'c'est la vie' attitude. Most of their spiritual "family" sympathized with him, at a loss what to say, but not Fran! She had taken such a beating in life and love that she pushed him around verbally until she got him laughing. Being close to the same age, nothing about him intimidated the saucy waitress. They began to develop a deep friendship and respect for one another as time went by. Erin and Allen concurred that it was good for both of them.

The time came when Laurie said she was ready. The coach offered to reserve the gym for her exclusive use for one hour on a Sunday. Since she wasn't sharing the spotlight with anyone else, that would be ample, she said. He did say word got around campus about what she was doing, generating a lot of interest. Since she han't objected to being watched, a number of faculty planned to attend, as well as many students that were involved within the athletics program,.

She said that was fine, it didn't bother her, but if they expected her to adhere to the rules like when she was trying to impress judges, they'd be disappointed. This was not about rules or competing. Those things held no interest for her. She wanted to show her new family the skills she had mastered, that was all. Anyone could sit in, but her family was to get the best seats on the sideline, 'cause this is for *them*, she declared. He laughingly agreed.

They told her they could be there in two weeks, if she liked. She consulted the coach, who scheduled her to have the gym from 1 to 2 p.m. Erin told her she was rescuing her since the weather was getting colder this time of year in her new home state! That cracked their girl up, who said she was glad to help. Erin would have no need for her parka in L.A. She made travel arrangements, then called Stef. Her partner said she'd have cameras ready to record Laurie's performance, also insisting they stay in her room at the house again. She was looking forward to seeing her best friends, she said!

Dani called and asked if she could talk to all of them, Heidi and Ruth included. When they were on the line, she said she had a vision of a door closing slowly, not yet shut. The opportunity to minister there was drawing to a close, she told them. Would they consider staying a bit longer this time?

Four women the Missourians hadn't met were working there now. The attitude in the house was changing, becoming colder. It wasn't time for her or Laurie to leave, she said, but it wouldn't surprise her if Emily gave notice. Nothing seemed to tie her there anymore. The Gypsy was melancholy, and often spoke of the place made for her longingly.

Dani still had her father to look after, sort of, in the facility nearby where Alzheimer's had driven him. He usually didn't recognize her, but hers was the only face he saw regularly relating to his former life. It was hard when he didn't know her, but she felt obligated to stay close by, in case he needed her.

Laurie wasn't free to leave either, though she wasn't sure why. Her little sister had some kind of unfinished business that was a mystery to her. She periodically spoke of moving to Missouri, but it wasn't eating at her like it was with Emily. The Lord was holding her desire at bay, for some reason. Dani was grateful, whatever the reason, saying it wouldn't be the same once Laurie was gone.

Their faith in Christ was increasingly isolating the four of them, Dani, Laurie, Emily, and Juanita, she said. Pam just listened when they talked about Him, and Stef tolerated it. Maggie's curiosity seemed to have vanished. Carmella dug back into her Catholic foundation, making it clear nothing they said interested her. Delilah had no use for any of that "nonsense." If not for Stef's personal ties to Erin, she suspected their reception would be much cooler than it had been. Well, besides the fact that Erin was the primary owner of the company employing them, she chuckled!

That does affect things, Erin agreed. Dani told them the new crop of wrestlers lacked the bond that had been so peculiar to the company before. She overheard Pam remark to Stef that when the 'three musketeers' left, the old camaraderie the staff used to enjoy would be gone with them. Stef just shrugged without answering.

Allen told Dani that when the love of Christ is rejected, the chill of death is what remains. The Lord would wrap up whatever the girls were there to do pretty soon, he was certain. When the time came, they would be ready for them with open arms, you included, little Sis, he promised. She liked that, she said!

When they prayed together about how long to stay this time, Ruth was set that they needed to plan to be there *the whole week* after Laurie's exhibition. It witnessed with all of them. Heidi declared God had something in the works requiring their presence for that amount of time, so they better pack for it! With their three trusted advisors in agreement on the matter, the couple chose not to question their counsel.

Erin pushed back the return tickets to accommodate

their extended stay, then texted the new plans to Stef with an offer to move to a motel after the first weekend. She texted back, "??? Talk later." Their entire fellowship was thrilled at the news, none more than their girls, Dani included. Her advice initiated the new plan, driving home how they valued her thoughts!

Two days before the couple flew out, news broke at the beginning of their conference call meeting. Carlos and Juanita announced they were expecting! Just like that, Juanita was out of wrestling. It was long-standing company policy pregnancy was cause to be removed from the active roster, rather than risk complications – and just good sense. They were excited, both sure his income could get them by.

They were showered with congratulations. Denise called babysitting privileges, followed by Fran, but Reina informed them the line formed behind her! Allen observed they'd have no shortage of volunteers, from the sound of it, which brought laughs.

CHAPTER 12

Erin and Allen returned to California nine weeks after the last visit on a Friday, late in the afternoon. They received a very warm welcome from their three girls, as usual. Surprisingly, Stef and Pam acted just as glad to see them! They were normally much more reserved.

Other greetings were unenthusiastic. The place seemed kind of gloomy. It was nearly 5 p.m., so Stef closed, dismissing everyone after making introductions with the new staff. Only the five of them stuck around.

"Did someone die here?" Erin asked no one in particular.

"It does kind of feel like it," Pam agreed, "but I couldn't tell you why. The new hires are competent but don't have the heart that used to draw us all together. It isn't just them, though. Of those who have worked here for years, these are the only ones who are a pleasure to be around. The rest just punch the clock, doing their time."

Stefanie's shoulders slumped. "Erin, normally I wouldn't talk in front of the employees, but none of these here are a problem. On the contrary, they have become the company's inspiration, like its heart and soul, but it doesn't seem to be enough. *I* can't seem to pull them together to make a team of them anymore, despite my best efforts. I organize things to keep us functional, but not really motivated. It's like I've lost my touch for management, somehow."

Dani spoke up, "That's not it, Stef. The old joy of being here is gone, like the whole place is depressed. Believe me, I *know* depression. How long has it been since anyone here laughed, other than us?"

Stef exchanged a look with Pam, "Weeks, I guess. You have a point. If we're not having fun, it just leaves us to carry out our duty." Her shoulders squared again as she nodded slowly, "Thanks, Dani. We'll bring the magic back by amusing ourselves while we work, the way we used to do. Guys won't know what hit 'em!" She went to her office to close out the day's business.

Pam looked at the rest as if trying to pierce their thoughts. "There's more to it than that, isn't there?" It was a statement, not really a question.

No one said anything, so Allen spoke. "Jesus said He is the way, the truth, and the life, Pam. He came here to offer that life for a brief time. Some received it," he waved toward the girls, "and the rest hardened their hearts. Now He is preparing to leave. Those who received His gift of life will follow Him."

"When life has departed, death is all that remains. Of those still here, you are the *only* one who appears to be giving Him a chance, but your window of opportunity is closing. You and Win need to decide whether you believe what He said, quickly. Stef does not. Remember Win's dream."

She stared at him like he had turned into the Grim Reaper! She actually *shivered* where she stood, then almost ran out the front door without a word. He realized he was being stared at from all angles.

"Dad?" Laurie whispered.

"What, honey?"

She heaved a sigh of relief, "For a minute there, you were *scary*."

The other two nodded, but Erin said, "No, girls, that wasn't him. For that moment, Jesus manifested through him to speak to Pam." Now their gaze focused on her in shock. "Jesus appeared to me when He saved my soul, remember? I'd recognize Him anywhere. I think He just pushed Pam off the fence."

Allen shrugged, "Maybe so. I hope so, but *she* will decide which side she lands on. Shall we go get some dinner? I'm hungry."

They did and Stef went along. Erin texted their friends they were back in town. After she fed her diabetic, they'd be at the house, if anyone wanted to see them. The girls were tickled to have them to themselves! Their joy seemed to rub off on Stef, once they left the house. Allen told Laurie she looked different somehow, maybe a little leaner. Smiling, she informed him two months of intensive training does that to a person.

There was a lot of smiling while they were out, but Emily's never seemed to rest. He called her on it, and inquired as to its cause. Her answer was blunt, "You. Both of you, really. I have missed you so much, while you were gone this time. It's like I don't belong here anymore, I belong with you. These sisters make being here bearable, but when I go home at night, I am alone. It's always kind of been like that for me. Gypsies are very social people, and I am an outcast.

"You are my new family. I have no words to express what that means to me! Now you have enlarged your home to make a place for me… All I want is to go there, be with you, and grandmother and Heidi; but at least you are here with me now, and I am so happy I can't stop smiling!" she giggled.

Stef looked at her seriously, "So what is keeping you here?"

Emily was caught by surprise, "I-I don't know. My sisters are still here, and I don't want to leave you short-handed, Stefanie. You and Erin have been good to me. I guess I feel obligated, to you and them, too."

Stef told her, "Life is short, Emily. Follow your heart! Many people never find their place in this world, but a special place has been made for you by the most wonderful people I know. I've hired plenty of help, so I'll be fine without you."

Dani stated, "Em, I'm here for my father. I can't go yet, not until I see how things turn out for him, but that has nothing to do with you. I value your friendship, but I'll still have that, even if you're not here, right?" Emily nodded emphatically.

Laurie weighed in, "Emily, go home! I won't be far behind you, believe me. I think Stef knows I've only put off giving notice until this exhibition for Dad is over."

Stef chuckled, "Yeah, I figured I'd be hearing from you on Monday. The only real surprise has been Juanita's news. I have coverage for all of you, at this point. Emily, if you give me notice now, maybe you can go with them when they leave in ten days."

Her face was alight, "One week would be enough?"

Stef laughed, "I'll manage, girl."

She looked at Erin and Allen. They nodded as she asked, "Could I go with you? Would that be okay? I guess I should pray about this."

He grinned, "So pray, we'll wait." Erin and Stef both laughed, but the younger ladies were shocked!

"Now?" she was incredulous.

"Why not?" he countered. "How long does it take you to ask God a question? His answer is obvious to us. Stefanie gave it to you."

Now the unbeliever in their midst looked surprised. He had her full attention as he continued. "You asked Jesus to come into your heart, right? He did that, and lives there now. The Bible says, *"The heart of the king is like the rivers of water; He turns it whithersoever He will."* He doesn't deal with kings any differently than the rest of us, since He is no respecter of persons.

"Everything in your heart, where Jesus sits on His throne inside you and speaks to you, is telling you to go home, daughter. Even your boss is telling you to follow your heart because she knows it's the right thing for *you.* No one else at this table has any doubt about it, other than you!"

She bowed her head briefly, then raised it with a look of excitement. She whirled to wrap Stefanie up in a full embrace, thanking her repeatedly. The older woman's expression was priceless, stunned and pleased simultaneously. She awkwardly returned the hug, saying thickly, "I'm gonna miss you, sweetheart."

Emily's excitement was contagious; even Stef wasn't immune. She blended right into the group after that. From what Allen could tell, she seemed to enjoy it, too. They finished dinner and headed back to the house, since some had responded to Erin's text to say they did plan to come see them. Their girls rode together to and from the restaurant, while Stef rode with the couple. She was quiet on the ride back but stopped them in the garage when they got out of the car.

"Allen, you told Emily my advice was the same as God's to her. How can that be? Are we alike that way, since I don't talk to Him?" she puzzled. Erin walked around the car to put an arm around him, grinning.

"Stef, you're a *lot* like Him, which isn't surprising, since He formed you in His image. You're a powerhouse, yet you don't push people around just because you could. That's how He is. He respects the wishes of people He could easily bully. He cares about all of us, instead.

"Your advice to Emily was spoken out of care for her, because you want her to be happy. You even waived a two-week notice for her so she could go home with us. You sacrificed that which you had every right to expect, out of kindness. A person who hasn't bowed the knee to Christ can still exhibit some of His best qualities. You have a good heart, making a pretty good case in point."

"Hmm," she seemed pleased.

"It won't get you into heaven, apart from Him," he pointed out, "but it makes you one heck of a lady, a person I'm proud to know and call a friend."

"*We're* proud to know and call a friend," Erin corrected him, causing the other two to grin.

Their hostess took their hands, "Thanks for that, guys. This outing with you has been just what the doctor ordered for me, a breath of fresh air. I'm glad you'll be around awhile, this time. Somehow, I don't feel so alone now." She waved them forward and they went in.

CHAPTER 13

Guillermo arrived first, bringing his boss from the bake shop. He introduced her as Carol, his mentor, and co-owner of the store where he worked. They had just dropped off a cake at a hotel for a symposium. She looked to be in her mid-forties, slightly stocky and cheerful. She wanted to meet Gui's friends. Though still in work clothes, they didn't act like they were in a hurry. He was respectful of her, while she seemed to regard him like a favored nephew. He introduced Erin, Allen, and Stef proudly.

Fran came in and hugged them close, also meeting Carol. She told them she worked the next day, so she came by to see them tonight. Laurie was informed she'd see her at the exhibition Sunday; she wouldn't miss *that* for the world! Gui stated his mom planned to be there, too, cheering her on. The expression on her face indicated she liked that news.

"You have no dearth of supporters, my girl," Allen declared with a chuckle, receiving a grin.

"That's the truth," Andrew echoed, having just come in.

"I'll be there, too, with bells on!" He got a long lingering hug from the big man, who then greeted everyone else before settling next to Fran. She ignored him for a moment, then dug her elbow into his ribs with a grin. He shook his head and returned the grin. Stef just looked like she was soaking in all the goodwill. An easy smile kept reappearing on her face.

They visited about nothing important, enjoying each other's company while getting acquainted with Carol. Erin updated them as texts came to her. Carlos and Juanita thought they'd make it, but it didn't work out, so they would see everyone tomorrow. Teresa would be bringing Alissa then, too. The teen said her parents would attend the exhibition Sunday, so they would meet them for the first time. Denise was at work, but planned to see them tomorrow.

When it became clear to everyone that all were present who were coming, Carol spoke up, not the least bit shy, "So let me see if I have this straight, okay? This is the lobby of a business built on the premise of women who wrestle and *defeat* men who *pay* for the experience, is that right?" Grinning nods were her reply. Shaking her head slowly, she uttered, "Wow. I had no idea that was a thing. Stefanie, you run this place?"

"You got it," Stef responded, "Erin and I are co-owners. I manage it since Erin retired. These three, Danielle, Emily, and Laurie all work here, with several other ladies not present at the moment. Gui's sister-in-law was working here, up until now."

She looked at her employee, "Your brother's new wife can kick his butt?"

"Oh, yes," his eyes went wide as he nodded emphatically, "and mine too, I expect. She's pretty tough!"

Several chuckled as she commented, "That's crazy. From what Gui tells me, though, the story gets crazier. The place is not a church, yet there is a sort of revival going on here where people are getting saved and set free from demons! I wouldn't have believed such a cockamamie rumor, but I know Guillermo. The change in him is unmistakable. He's not gay anymore. That's not something they can just turn off!"

"You're right about that," Allen agreed, "They don't control the lusts, the lusts control them. I take it you have some church background, Carol?"

She nodded, "I do. I'm Methodist, was raised Methodist since childhood. I've seen people receive Christ and get saved, but I've *never* seen anyone delivered from demons or a gay lifestyle. I didn't know that kind of thing still happened."

He half expected Stef to excuse herself, but a glance her way made him aware she was interested in this. It seemed to amuse her another Christian didn't understand happenings that took place so close to her. She caught his look her way; he realized she was waiting to see his response.

He leaned forward, "First, I want to say I admire your heart, Carol. I really mean that. Knowing Gui was gay, you still took him under your wing, giving him the training he needed to become the artist he is today. The cake he made for his brother's wedding was breathtaking!" The whole room was in agreement. Gui grinned at the rave review of his handiwork.

"A lot of churchgoing folks would shy away from gays, wanting nothing to do with the sin that traps them. The gay community paints that as prejudice, and for legalists it is, with their "holier than thou" attitude; but many others fear proximity to sin will contaminate them, so they withdraw. Those who know where they stand in Christ comprehend they cannot bear witness of Him to sinners if they keep them at a distance. Obviously, that hasn't escaped you."

She sat back, relaxed, and smiled. "A lot of people in our congregation don't understand why my husband and I don't separate ourselves from sinners more than we do. If we did, we'd go broke! We've been praying for this young man ever since he came to us, while also trying to live what we believe. He seemed to respect us, rather than resent our differences. We couldn't have worked side by side, otherwise. The only tension I've noticed is when we're pushing to meet a deadline."

Gui spoke up, "Yeah, and we're pretty good, even in those circumstances." Chuckling, she nodded.

"So you were praying for Gui because you care about him, which means you believe God answers prayer. It sounds like the idea He provided deliverance doesn't really startle you, just how and where He did it, outside and apart from your church. Is that the gist of your curiosity?"

She thought a moment, "I guess that's most of it. I wonder what he found here that made such a difference. What do you have that we don't?"

"In a word, *power*," he told her directly. "I know that sounds like bragging, but it's not. It doesn't come from us, we just receive what Christ provides. Relatively few believers do that, because we all struggle with some unbelief. One of the most common claims Christians have is that we believe the Bible in its entirety. It would be more accurate to say that *we want to*, since the truth is none of us really do, no matter how hard we try.

"There are parts of God's word that stagger our imagination; we struggle to take it in. Add to that the serpent of Eden still questioning it, "Hath God *really* said...?" and it ends up watered down to something more easily accepted, but devoid of power. The more the Bible is explained and reworded, rather than accepted at face value, the less power it has to change lives." Movement caught his eye, as Stef rose and silently left the room.

"What are you getting at, Allen? I do believe the Bible," she was offended, and sat up straight.

"I'm sure you do, Carol, to the best of your

understanding. Would you say you understand it perfectly?"

"Well, no, I can't say that. Do you think you do?"

He laughed, "Not on your life, sister! I'm far from perfect. I wouldn't even say I have a better grasp of scripture than you do. Even if I did, how would I know? That would be a very foolish boast. Still, there are certain truths each of us has laid hold of that could benefit the other, don't you think?"

"Okay, I'll agree to that," she allowed.

"You said you didn't know deliverance still happened, yet you believed God would answer your prayers on Gui's behalf, somehow. You went to the Lord in faith, even though your experience gave you no cause to expect results. He honored your prayer of faith, yet not in the way you expected. You are praising Him for what He has done and He is stretching you outside your comfort zone because He wants you to grow in that faith. Your curiosity brought you to meet us because what we have received can benefit you if you'll receive it, too."

"The Holy Spirit," Dani breathed. He just smiled at her.

"I'm listening," Carol prompted him.

"I'm sure you're familiar with the Great Commission." She nodded. *"Go ye into all the world...,"* He said, then instructed them to tarry in Jerusalem first, until they were imbued with power from on high. That happened on the Day of Pentecost, according to the book of Acts.

"From that day forward, they were empowered to do all the works Jesus did in His ministry. It wasn't just the twelve, either. Many others manifested mighty miracles afterward because they received the Holy Spirit Jesus promised to send them. Several denominations nowadays teach that this doesn't happen anymore, but I have yet to find scripture backing up that view.

"Jesus said He is the same yesterday, today, and forever. If He furnished the early church a Comforter to sustain them in His absence who worked in such powerful ways to validate His gospel, why would He treat us differently? Gui's new liberty, and for that matter, the fact that I am still alive and sitting here visiting with you, are strong evidence Jesus' tactics haven't changed a bit!"

"So you're Pentecostal, then," she stated.

He shook his head, "Not exactly. I grew up in those churches, Pentecostal, Foursquare, and Assembly of God, but I don't fit with any of them now. I'd be an outsider at any of them because I don't adhere to their teachings. I bottomed out in life a long time ago and called out to Christ, one last-ditch cry for help before committing suicide. He met me.

"That changes anyone, Carol. He sustains me now, whether I'm in a church or outside all of them. When you can pin down a denomination Jesus confesses is His own, that will be mine, because I follow Him. I have no life apart from Him.

"In the book of Revelation, He addresses seven different churches. None of them are perfect before Him, but He has some in every one, at least a few. He also gathers us from the highways and byways. His sheep hear His voice, coming to Him wherever He finds us. We are bound to Him and will follow Him anywhere, sometimes into a church, sometimes out of one. If we love one another as He has loved us, He will gather more to us, because we are surrounded by hurting people who value our love.

"That's how we have come together. We're not a church, so to speak. We're just folks who were hurting that have been transformed by His love, drawn together by this tie that has become part of us to make us a new kind of family, united in Him; and we're helping each other recover from those hurts. It only works because He is in our midst."

The silence was deafening. A few had tears streaking their cheeks. Carol noticed. "You *might* be wrong, but you're definitely not phony," she said quietly. "May I ask what hurt you are recovering from, Allen?"

Erin took his hand as they exchanged a smile, "A 38-year marriage gone south. She decided the grass was greener elsewhere. This incredible woman, a pioneer in the fine art of dismantling men, is assisting Jesus in putting me back together. She has splinted my broken heart with her own, ever since the Lord brought her to me in Missouri. There's no separating us now."

"38 years? It's insane to walk away from that!" she was exasperated.

"I think so, too," Erin concurred, "but Allen led me to Christ. I'd still be lost in sin, otherwise, so I have to believe God meant it for good. Other than Fran, those here, and some not here at the moment, all trace their salvation to the things God has done since He brought Allen and me together.

"He never would have come here to bear witness of God's grace, had the Lord not brought us together first. We may be new to life in Christ, but His sovereignty over bad circumstances has been driven home to us already. And this man who thought he'd never be loved again has been hemmed in on every side by people who love him dearly, *especially me!*" Cheers, laughter, and clapping rose to reinforce her statement.

CHAPTER 14

Like everyone else, Andrew sat quietly to this point, but now he spoke up, "Carol, you said Allen might be wrong. How about let's find out? My man hasn't steered me wrong yet! I haven't received the baptism of the Holy Spirit. It kind of stretched my imagination to think of praying in tongues, but everyone else here does it, so what's the harm in asking God for it?"

His gaze settled on Allen's partner, "Besides, Erin told me the longer I put it off, the more I'd kick myself. I've learned the hard way not to doubt *anything* that little lady says!" Several cracked up laughing, Erin among them. Andrew broke into a big grin, "Are you with me, sister?"

She took a deep breath, "Why not? Let's lay this thing to rest before God. I can pray, as far as that goes. Allen, is there anything we should do first?"

He shook his head, "Not that I know of. We'll bow our heads and pray silently, so as not to interfere. If you stand to ask for God's gift, would you object to Gui standing with you?"

Andrew shook his head. Carol smiled, "Of course not!" Gui was surprised, but rose with them, looking at Allen.

He directed him to stand between them, taking the hand of each. "Gui, you just pray in tongues aloud, but quietly, okay? The rest of us will pray with you silently." He nodded, then Allen gestured toward Carol.

All bowed their heads. She began to recite the Lord's Prayer, sounding formal. The unexpectedness of hearing it being recited caused him to look up momentarily. He noted Andrew's lips were moving too, but not synchronized with her prayer. He was offering up his own. Gui was barely audible, praying in tongues. His eyes closed again until she completed her recitation.

She added a single request, "Heavenly Father, if there is any other gift you would bestow on us, in addition to all Your Holy Son has provided for our redemption, please forgive my stubbornness in waiting so long to receive it. Jesus..." She launched into tongues and her eyes opened wide! It was plain she was trying to regain control of her speech, but it wasn't happening; she just got louder. Andrew went into tongues, too, punctuated by laughter that ended up with tears of joy running down his face.

Gui released their hands, and clapped Andrew's arm with a chuckle, "It's good, ain't it, brother?"

Andrew laughed, and nodded, "Yes, it is!" he spoke between praises.

Fran stepped up to put an arm around Carol, "Don't fight it, honey. You offered your lips to the Lord and He accepted your offering! Just thank Him, don't try to take it back." The tension went out of the older woman as she digested that. Praises began to be heard among the unintelligible utterance coming forth. They were all on their feet at that point, praises, thanksgiving, and laughter pouring forth from them. The Lord's presence was joy in their midst!

As things started to die down, Andrew stepped forward

with another laugh to wrap Allen up in one of his huge hugs, "You weren't wrong, Allen! God is *so good!*" He just laughed, holding him the best he could.

When he released him, he found Carol staring at him as though seeing him for the first time. He grinned, "Well, what do you think?"

She grinned back, *"That –* was unprecedented. I finally get why David danced before the Lord, the sheer delight he must have felt in His presence. I'm not just a Methodist anymore," she chuckled.

"Then you get why I said I'm not just a Pentecostal anymore," he pointed out, "which is okay since we're Christ's now more than ever before."

She nodded, her eyes alight, "That's true. I plan to go home and ruin my Methodist husband, too!" That cracked everyone up.

He went over how the Spirit teaches and reminds those who embrace Him of scripture. He puts words in their mouths to make their witness more effective, also directing them in unfamiliar situations. He emphasized how praying in tongues works like a 'panic button' when they're afraid or uncertain. He works *with* them, not forcing His will on them, convicting rather than subjugating.

Andrew soaked it up. Carol recognized the scriptures he referenced, but their meaning came through in a way they never had before. She said she was going to study these things anew with this fresh perspective. Erin and the girls invited her to join the daily fellowships, as well. She and Gui had to leave after that. He signaled a thumbs-up on the way out, with a grin. It hit Allen that was the reason he brought her there!

When the Lord moves among His people, there is a kind of 'afterglow' that makes them want to linger with each other where He met them. They settled to visit some more. Allen was shaking his head at the notion Gui brought Carol to them to receive the Holy Spirit, a little half-smile on his face. Emily asked what had him amused, so he told them what he believed Gui's thumbs-up indicated, which got several chuckles.

Dani nodded, "That fits with some of the things Juanita has described about him, Allen. She said he is a schemer and a prankster. He probably wanted to break through that religious propriety she came here with, figured if anyone could do it, the Holy Spirit could. The rotten scamp! She sure got blessed out of it, though."

"Me, too," Andrew rumbled. He looked at Erin, "You were right, I shouldn't have hesitated to ask for that baptism, but I do feel like tonight was appointed. It took Carol off the spot when I stood with her to ask for God's gift."

She responded, "I think so, too. I hesitated, then kicked myself afterward, but the truth is Heidi was so blessed and moved when the gift came through her hands, I think that was divinely appointed, too. I guess we ought to stop reflecting on our failings so much, and focus on God's marvelous timing, instead. You did good, Andrew." He grinned.

Fran took Andrew's hand, sitting beside her, then locked her gaze on Erin's mate. "Allen, do you realize the measure of trust Gui has in you, to do what he did? Once again, you did not disappoint. You won him over every bit as much as his brother, who was so impressed with you that he insisted *you* marry him and Juanita. Even you can't have missed how extraordinary that was!

"This big teddy bear beside me thinks just as highly of you, too, obviously. We ladies love you – I think you know that – but if you're tempted to think we're just overly emotional women, how do you explain the way these guys have gravitated to you? You are a very special man, and don't you forget it, understand?"

The lump in his throat made it hard to speak, but he croaked out, "Thank you."

Erin caught his chin, turning his head to face her. Her eyes were moist, a crooked grin on her face, "Don't worry, we won't let you forget, will we, girls?" Laughing agreement and sniffles affirmed her declaration. He was speechless, and just hugged his Genie close, trying to keep it together.

Andrew chuckled, "Allen, I think Fran is trying to make a point to all these tough ladies here, that she can make a grown man cry *without* hurting him."

A loud snort came from her, followed by his "Oof!" as he took an elbow to the ribs, drawing giggles from the spectators. Allen couldn't help but laugh, looking at the indignant waitress dwarfed by the giant trying to guard his ribs.

"Don't sell her short, Andrew," he warned him. "My tears may be painless, but if you're not careful, yours won't be!"

"Tell me about it," he moaned, rubbing his side tenderly. "I'm taking abuse here!"

"Then quit picking on me," she advised him with a smirk.

"I wasn't picking on you," he objected, "just trying to help my man Allen keep it together by giving him a laugh. It's a bro thing, okay?"

"I appreciate that, but it's not worth putting yourself in harm's way," the elder man advised him. "Besides, these ladies have seen me cry and they don't make fun of me. They're very considerate."

Fran mellowed, "I have to admit, that was thoughtful of you too, Andrew. Sorry about the elbow."

"Thank you," he told her, smiling.

Those two left soon after that, Dani a short bit later. Laurie and Emily lingered, as Stef rejoined them, fresh from a workout and shower. Erin mentioned ice cream; that's all it took to motivate an outing! When they got back, the girls departed. Having Stef alone, the couple wondered aloud if their extended visit would be more convenient for her if they rented a motel room. She told them their company more than made up for the inconvenience, but she'd let them know if she needed her space. Fair enough, they said.

She asked why they were planning to stick around. Did they have some specific reason? That was a little tougher to explain, but they tried to tell her they felt like they'd be needed, somehow.

She nodded, "Gotcha. I learned a long time ago when I have a hunch about something, it's a bad idea to ignore it. I totally understand. Let's see what develops over the coming week, then." They didn't consider the Lord's direction the same as a "hunch", but were glad she didn't write them off as flaky, so they left it at that.

CHAPTER 15

The next day was enjoyable, hanging out with their West Coast friends after the morning Bible study. Erin led a movement culminating with Juanita finally making the tacos her husband raved about. She tried to back out, using the excuse she was pregnant, but it didn't work Stef told her it got her out of wrestling, but that's all. It's no reason to get lazy! Besides, she would kick herself if she didn't stay in shape. She might not be her boss now, but she was still her friend. Friends don't let friends neglect their health!

Carlos was told that despite his inclination to pamper her, he better not go overboard, and let Stef know if his girl got too soft. She'd put an end to that! He was amused, telling Juanita now he had something to hold over her head! She laughingly said that was okay, but he better not go nuts, because pregnancy isn't permanent and paybacks would follow!

Carlos hadn't embellished his wife's cooking in the slightest. Her tacos were incredible! Everyone raved about them until she began to be embarrassed. He put them away like they were candy, again making Allen wonder how he was not obese. He wasn't the only one to notice, either.

Dani told Stef in front of everyone that if she wanted to make sure Juanita wasn't getting lazy, keep an eye on her husband. If he started putting on weight, it was evidence she wasn't helping him burn off the calories! They laughed and laughed. The couple was red-faced and speechless, finally giving way to guilty little smiles. Allen was grateful Alissa hadn't arrived with Teresa yet, chiding Dani for her adult humor. She assured him she wouldn't have said it if the teen had been present.

The day was relaxing. They hung around the house, visiting with everyone who came to see them, folks coming and going as they wished. A grill was put to use in the backyard that produced all kinds of treats in the late afternoon, hot dogs, hamburgers, chicken, ribs, and even shish kabobs. Potatoes and carrots were wrapped in foil and thrown on the grill as sides, while an endless supply of tossed salad was being devoured.

Reina brought a croquet set with her that was put to good use. Those who had played mini golf with Laurie were a little nervous when she had a mallet in her hands. Grinning, she gave them a razzberry. Their worries were baseless. She never made the balls fly.

The grill was managed by Stef and Dani, obviously not for the first time. Carlos offered his help, too. He was a long-time griller, it turned out. They joked he and his girl could keep them fed anytime. The door was always open to skills like theirs!

Stef went in a bit before 5 p.m. to get ready to leave. She had plans that would take her away overnight but promised Laurie she would not miss her program the next day. A few faces popped in they had not seen since the first visit at their belated "reception", old friends of Erin and two or three former employees. At about 6 p.m., Pam and Win showed up as Dani began to shut down the grill. Enough had been cooked they were able to enjoy their fill, while the guests started filtering out into the night.

Once the gathering dwindled down to only faces familiar to them, Win began to address him. "Allen, our visit tonight isn't just social. It's related to the investigation you suggested Pam and I undertake together into the claims of Christ. By the way, thanks for recommending Mark's Gospel. We completed it without getting bogged down, the way we had with John. It's been a topic of discussion for us ever since."

Pam swallowed, "*I* discussed it, into the ground. I've been a very hard sell, truth be told. Win has been more thorough than I thought possible, researching surviving records of the Roman Empire for references to Jesus of Nazareth. He found a surprising number of them. Apparently, their bureaucracy generated a lot of recordkeeping.

"Those records tend to back up scripture, unintentionally. Some of it, like shepherds coming in from the fields to see the newborn babe, was a matter of public record, also referred to in Luke's gospel. Things like that didn't normally happen, so people took notice." Those around them were riveted, this being news to them.

Pam was abashed, "Win was convinced about Jesus before I was. I was still – hesitating – when you told me my window of opportunity was closing. It was like you were inside my head, telling me to make up my mind! It scared me. I didn't think any man could do that, especially one as mild-mannered as you. Then I realized it couldn't be you; it had to be *Jesus in you*, challenging me. Only He could address my thoughts, which gave me the answer I was pursuing. He *is* real!"

Win spoke again, with a sheepish smile. "Our point is, we're ready to receive Him now if He'll accept us." He grasped Pam's hand.

She added, "Both of us are, at last."

Erin chuckled, "Welcome to my world, Pam. Every time I'd get comfortable thinking I had Allen figured out when we were courting, *Jesus* would show through him and knock my perspective reeling! It didn't stop until I asked Him into my heart."

He led them in a simple sinner's prayer:

"Lord Jesus, I believe You are God's Son, come in the flesh. I am a sinner.

Please have mercy on me! You died on the cross as a sinless sacrifice to atone

for my sins. Your blood washes me clean. God raised You from the dead

because You are innocent and righteous; forgive me, that I might live with

You, forever in Your kingdom. Come into my heart and I will live for You from

now on, my Lord and my God. Thank You for loving me so much! Amen."

Clapping broke out, raw excitement finding an outlet in applause to the Lord with praise and thanksgiving! A look of wonder appeared on Pam's face. Win sat back with a sigh of relief, more relaxed than Allen had ever seen him. Exchanging a look, they said together simultaneously, "It's gonna be okay now!" They broke out laughing.

Pam asked, "What was that?"

Win grinned, "I don't know, but I know it's true. Ever since my dream, I had this sense of foreboding doom, but it's gone now. It's gonna be okay with us, I just know it!"

"You're right," she agreed with a smile. "It's the strangest thing, but I know that's right!"

Allen grinned, "Pam, *that's* your inheritance from Uncle Al. It's the supernatural comfort he received from the Lord, then passed on to you. As soon as you came to Christ, He pulled it up over you like a blanket, because now you rest in Him. Win is being comforted too, because He is so near to you."

She shook her head, amazed, "That crazy, sweet old man! I never dreamed he could bequeath something like this. How did he do it?"

"God permitted him to do so; it's the only way a human could pass on a spiritual blessing. God comforted him by promising he would have an heir to whom he could pass on whatever he valued. He valued his faith, his Bible, and the blessing the Lord bestowed on him. You couldn't use his faith – you needed your own to come to Christ – but he left the rest to you. Only someone whose heart belonged to Jesus could benefit from the blessing."

"No wonder he didn't leave it to Delilah! He didn't believe it would help her at all, especially since she continues to refuse Christ!"

"You got it," he confirmed.

"Whoa! Time out!" Andrew declared. He was shocked! "Somebody *knew* Delilah would refuse to accept God? Why wasn't I told upfront? You could have spared me a lot of pain!" He was looking right at Allen.

"How?" he asked, point-blank. "God didn't reveal that to any of us. Her Uncle Al had prayed for her salvation *all her life*. It moved God's heart because He knew Delilah's. God knew she wouldn't have Him, so He showed her uncle, gifting this dispensation of peace to comfort him. He also promised him an heir to pass it on to, and that Delilah would bring him that heir.

"She brought Pam with her on her final visit to see Al. The old fellow recognized God was keeping His promise, so he told Pam where he stood, holding nothing back. You just watched her get saved, Andrew! At the time, she thought he was addled."

"I get that, Allen. I don't fault her at all, but how could *you* know about this and not tell me?" Clearly, he felt Allen had betrayed him.

Erin spoke, "Andrew, you don't know the whole story.

Pam, would you bring him current on everything pertaining to this, including how we got involved? It's your testimony to tell, anyway. We kept silent about what you told us because it was personal, so what you say will be news to everyone else here, too. Sharing our testimonies of what Christ has done for us is a way we can give back to Him, also bonding us to one another in the process."

Pam agreed, beginning with meeting Allen for the first time at their "reception". Relating how Erin stood with him as he prayed for the Lord to bring her and Delilah the mates He would provide for them, *two* jaws dropped in surprise. Win knew nothing about that prayer, either. Their girls did, though, and were spellbound.

She emphasized how the prayer impacted her, so totally outside her experience. Delilah mentioned how it reminded her of her uncle, "the happiest man she had ever known." The description intrigued her, so when her carpooling buddy invited her along to go visit him, she was up for it. Uncle Al was welcoming, kind, and intelligent in their short visit, cleverly setting up a way he could talk to her privately without his niece present.

When she couldn't dismiss his request for her to call him, it quickly became apparent just how intelligent he was! He spoke of his faith as a matter of fact, not trying to convert her, but rather informing her of his perspective. Identifying her as the heir God promised him, he bequeathed the blessing he had been given to comfort him when he learned his beloved niece would *not* receive Christ, no matter how much he prayed for her. Because she would not value Him, the old man said, neither would she value anything He provided – including Andrew. He predicted she would reject him.

"I'm sorry, Andrew," she told him softly. "I didn't know what to make of Uncle Al back then. He sounded a little cracked, to me. If I knew then what I know now, I would have warned you about her, I think."

The big man's eyes were moist, "Aww, I can't fault you, Pam. What could you do with *that*? Neither one of us trusted Jesus at the time."

She nodded, "That's it. I wasn't sure if He was real. If it helps, Al also said you'd be better off without her, that God had something better for you. I had not met Win at the time; I was wondering if I would see any answer to the prayer offered up for me. Turns out I just had to wait a little longer for my gift." She smiled at Win, who grinned. "Maybe it's the same for you."

He had a small smile as he nodded agreement. Her story went on, as she continued with how Al predicted Delilah would betray her. He died two days later. She attended his funeral, though his niece chose not to, and was given his Bible as a result. His inscription indicated *he knew* that would be the case, too. Heads shook in amazement on hearing of it.

Not having read the inscription yet, she readily relinquished it to Delilah on request the next morning. It appeared she had a change of heart, after showing no interest in claiming it the night before. When the boy approached her after her run to return it to her, having witnessed her coworker toss it into a dumpster, he inquired if her name was written on it. Remembering the crazy old man, she thought it just might be, so she checked and found the inscription. The boy was gone when she looked up again.

Of all who came to Christ through their witness in California so far, only Fran and Carol were not present. (Technically, they were saved before Erin and Allen met them.) Their little family was completely absorbed in Pam's tale, on the edge of their seats. It would have taken a fire alarm to move them, at that point!

Rattled at all that transpired, Pam read Laurie's text announcing their plan to return, then spontaneously decided to confide in them. She spoke of her call, and how Allen put events in perspective for her. When she said he postulated the boy who returned the Bible might well be an angel in disguise, there were gasps!

"God still does that?" Reina wanted to know.

"I am the Lord; I change not," he reminded her, "That's what His Word says. Pam, if that book had not been returned to you, would you and Win be sitting here with us tonight, having just invited Jesus into your hearts?"

She shook her head and looked at Win, who shook his. "I doubt it, Allen. We wouldn't have bought one." She chuckled, "I only kept Al's because of how it came to me. It was a personal gift, Al's dying wish, and it wouldn't go away!" They all laughed.

CHAPTER 16

"God does what it takes to bring His beloved home to Him," Allen told the room, and Reina in particular. "Aren't you glad He loves us enough to do that?" There were enthusiastic nods around the room, with several "Amens".

He fixed Win with his gaze. "I'm going to cap off Pam's story by telling on her, Win." The dentist leaned forward, grinning, but she looked confused, apparently not sure what Allen would say. "When Al said Delilah had rejected Christ, therefore would not value His gifts to her, he also made a statement about Pam. He said she would treasure the gifts He offered her. Something to think about; could you stand to be treasured?"

He sat back, speechless, looking at Pam. She nodded. His eyes welled with tears. She clasped his hand with both of hers, then glanced at Allen irritably. "Will you stop putting him on the spot?!"

Andrew gave a rumbling laugh, "My man is just broaching what all of us guys wonder, but are afraid to ask, Pam. We are scared jackrabbits at the thought we might be rejected, though we try to bluff otherwise. He is reassuring Win, or trying to, in his own way. He couldn't do it if Erin wasn't building his confidence. I'm pretty sure he knows you'll do the same for Win."

Erin hooked her arm through Allen's, then smiled at him and nodded, pleased. He cleared his throat, "I don't mean to put anyone on the spot, guys. Sorry if I come across that way. A man in his forties who never found love isn't likely to be very sure of himself. I know the feeling all too well. In my own goofy way, Pam, I'm trying to let my brother in Christ know I consider you *trustworthy*."

She inclined her head, "Oh! Well, thank you! In that case, if you're not trying to embarrass him, be my guest!" That brought chuckles.

Andrew spoke, "Allen, I'm sorry. I see now you couldn't have spared me. I was involved with Delilah before we even met. That involvement was how we met. Since then, even though I lost her, I gained Christ and all of you! I'm not with anyone, but I'm not alone anymore, either. That's hugely comforting to me."

Dani jumped in, "Join the club, big fellow! That's exactly where we're at, right now. Believe me, it isn't by choice, but it's *wonderful* to have this close family around us while we wait for the partners God is preparing for each of us."

"Preach it, sister!" Laurie exclaimed. It got everyone laughing. They visited into the evening, getting better acquainted. Win and Pam seemed very comfortable becoming part of their circle, and said they would be glad to take part in their conference call gatherings.

Laurie got up to give Pam a hug, pointing out that with Emily leaving, it would be very nice to have a coworker to stand with her and Dani in faith. Dani agreed wholeheartedly, wishing Stef would come to Christ, too. "All we can do is pray," Erin told her soberly. Alissa also asked them to pray for her family's salvation. They decided to agree in prayer for all of them. The Lord's comfort was present in response, setting their hearts at rest.

The visit continued until Allen yawned, amusing everyone. "I'm still on Central Time," he stated in his defense.

"Jet lag will make a pretty good excuse, too," Win offered helpfully.

Teresa added insult to injury when she stood, saying it was time to go so the old man could get to bed! His jaw dropped, but before he could respond, Reina yawned. That brought lots of laughter, especially from her.

"I guess you're not the only one that needs some rest, Allen," she admitted.

"*Thank you,* Reina! Old man, indeed!" he objected, then yawned again, nullifying his indignation and bringing more laughter. His girls made a show of pitying him. He realized there was no salvaging his dignity.

Alissa had the giggles, along with Denise. Laurie and Juanita were getting there, quickly. Allen stuck out his tongue at all of them, bidding them to go home if all they were going to do was laugh at him! His grin took the sting out of it, though.

When they were saying goodnight, he did get some satisfaction as others drew a share of the laughter. Gui yawned, then Erin, and finally Andrew. It was a merry band of people that left that evening! Taking Erin's hand, he invited her to come lay with him, so they could *yawn* at each other. She cracked up, but didn't refuse the invitation!

Sunday morning they had Bible study/devotions by phone, with a special prayer for Laurie, that she would be blessed in her efforts and avoid injury. It touched her. There was excitement in the air for her exhibition. She received plenty of encouragement. Something else became apparent to Allen in prayer, though. He didn't speak of it to anyone until they got off the phone.

Erin picked up on it. He thought how he'd hate to try to

keep a secret from her! She just seemed to know when something was on his mind.

"Did God show you something, Sweet Talker?"

He grinned, "Nothing gets past you, does it?"

Stepping up to him, she put her arms around his neck, the old wolfish smile filling his view, "Not when it comes to you, love. I guard my heart, so anything that touches you is worth my notice. What is our King telling you?"

"I can't say, for sure. I get the impression this is going to be another divine appointment, you know?" His arms were around her, holding her close. "He's going to do something powerful at this event. It may be *Laurie's* exhibition, but something of Christ's sovereignty is going to be displayed, too. I have no idea how."

"I like the sound of that," she grinned, then kissed him.

He stared at her, "Your eyes are so beautiful! How do I ever manage to look away from them?"

She giggled, and gave him a deep kiss. "For one thing, there is more to me than eyes, my dear man. The rest of me deserves appreciation, too. Besides, there are other things in life you need to see, or you'd be walking into walls! Don't worry, when you have to look away, I'll still be here with you, so you can turn your gaze back on me whenever you like. Think of me as a magnet for your eyes!"

"Boy, is that the truth!" Another giggle escaped her. "You're more than eye candy, Genie; you're a *feast* for mine!"

They arrived thirty minutes early for the exhibition and got seated. A few students were just clearing out. He wasn't sure what they had been doing, but they were sweating. People dotted the bleachers here and there, settling in. Ropes cordoned off a small section of the front three rows in the middle, with signs posted, "Special Guests." They established their place on the front row, in the center.

Fran and Denise arrived minutes later, greeting them before sitting down. Fran was flushed, announcing

"Something good is going to happen here today!" Erin and her man exchanged a grin. Noticing, Fran grinned, too, "You know, don't you?"

"I've had the same impression, ever since we prayed," he told her, "but I have no clue why. All I know is this is somehow closure for our girl. Twice now, you have confirmed what He indicated to me, Fran. Seems to me a pattern is developing!"

She was very pleased with his observation. "What does that mean, Allen?"

"Well, you're sensitive to the Holy Spirit, for one thing. It ought to build your confidence! For another, you and I can check each other for accuracy, helping prevent mistakes we might regret. We have three advisors to give us wise counsel, but if I can rely on someone to supply confirmation in spiritual matters, someone secure enough in their faith to confront me when I'm wrong, that's very comforting. You validate me, without even trying. I'm not perfect, Fran, but when you check me, I feel like I don't have to be. Does that make sense?"

She nodded, "It does. I'm not perfect either, not by any stretch, but comparing notes with someone you trust goes a *long* way toward minimizing the fear of failure. Those of us who have failed before need that."

"Yeah, we do. You keep checking me, okay?" She nodded. Denise smiled at her friend. "I don't think that's the extent of your contribution to this family, though. The Lord is grooming you for something more. You'll grow into whatever it is. He can make spectacular use of the most broken vessels, so stand by! It will be a pleasure to watch what He does with you!" Tears coursed down her cheeks, but a smile lit her face.

Denise had pulled out a pad the size of her hand, and was writing furiously. They watched with curiosity until she tore out the paper and gave it to Fran, who shook her head and grinned.

Denise smiled, "One advantage to being a waitress is developing good short-term memory. I wrote down what you said, so she can refer back to it. That kind of encouragement deserves to be remembered, don't you think?" Fran hugged her.

He nodded, amazed at the insight. Erin told her, "You're onto something, sweetie. You keep doing that, okay? Take notes of whatever passes you consider noteworthy. Human memory being as fallible as it is, what God says and does in our midst really should be recorded. Will you be our record keeper?" Fran nodded enthusiastically.

Denise was surprised, "Really? I've been wondering how I could contribute. You think *this* would matter? Erin, this is the easiest thing in the world for me!"

Others were coming in, so the conversation got sidelined. Stef arrived, also Carlos, Juanita, Reina, Guillermo, and Andrew. Nearly all the employees of A*C*E came in, even three of the four new hires. Two camera operators were present by then. Stef issued brief instructions concerning the coverage she wanted. Seasoned pros, that was all they needed.

Carol introduced her husband Tom before being seated near Gui. Teresa arrived with her husband and waved at them before sitting down. Win, Pam, Dani, and Emily came in with minutes to spare. Alissa brought her family to meet them: her dad, Hans; her mom, Alma; and her little brother, Erik. They were polite and friendly, but reserved. They insisted on sitting outside the reserved space.

The bank of bleachers was three-quarters full, just before Laurie came out. They were not expecting such a turnout for an unofficial event displaying the talents of an athlete not enrolled in the university!

A tall man in his late thirties came out with a microphone in his hand, striding directly up to Erin and Allen. He shook Erin's hand with a big grin, introducing himself as Coach Radburn. Erin introduced her husband.

He was very glad to meet him, he said; the man who coaxed Laurie out of retirement for this show and wedded the toughest woman ever to kick his butt! Erin chuckled. He said he hoped they'd get a chance to talk after it was over, then stepped back to address the crowd.

Turning on the microphone, he began. "Ladies and gentlemen, on behalf of the staff and faculty of our institution, I have the occasional honor to present a guest into our midst who is willing and able to display true greatness in his or her specialty. Such is the case today. She has retired from gymnastics for personal reasons, but those she holds dear have prevailed on her to exhibit her mastery for their appreciation – and ours – one last time."

"There are no judges to impress. She has nothing to prove. This is a gracious display of athleticism second to none, in my opinion, and I've been around the block enough to know when I see excellence! Please welcome Laurie Parcille!"

Laurie entered from an alcove, wearing a lavender leotard. She waved at the crowd with a grin as she walked up to the coach. She said something, then he handed her the microphone.

She spoke briefly, "Coach Radburn is very kind. My thanks to the university for the use of the facilities, both today and in the previous weeks while I was shaking off the rust. Allen and Erin, would you please stand?" They did, smiling at her. "Since I lost my mom and dad, these two have taken their place in my heart. No one but Jesus Christ means more to me now! I hope the rest of you enjoy my performance, but Mom, Dad... this is for *you*! I love you!"

CHAPTER 17

Handing the mike back to the coach, she went to the uneven bars. He followed after a moment while she powdered her hands. Hoisting her up until she got her grasp, he then retreated quickly.

Laurie pulled herself straight up until her waist was even with the bar, then folded her body over it into a flip that gave her instant momentum. She began to swing in full circles, once, twice; the third time she turned so she was swinging backward. She folded at the waist to hook the bar behind her knees. Stopping at the top of the swing to grab the bar with her hands, she extended her full length straight up to pause, motionless!

In slow motion, she did the splits upside down, then folded at the waist, bringing her feet under her knees. Lowering herself incrementally using only her arms, her feet touched the bar. At that moment, she swung as though she had lost her balance, but at the top of the next swing, she sprang to the high bar!

The crowd cheered. Paying no attention, Laurie spun

ever faster like a dervish, turning until she flew loose into the air. She held her knees to her chest in a kind of monkey flip that caught the low bar again. There was clapping, but Allen couldn't look away. It absolutely amazed him. No wonder the girl could bend horseshoes, doing stunts like this, he thought!

At the second swing on the low bar, she released her grip to go flying backward *over* the high bar, catching it in her hands at the last second! There was a collective gasp, followed by more applause. A backward somersault in midair took her to the low bar, then two swings led to a leap back again. Three fully extended giant swings ended in a dismount that looked like a wobbling kind of corkscrew flip, but the way she stuck the landing proved there was no lack of control in what she did!

He found out later the whole crowd was on their feet, clapping. *He was*, his jaw hanging open. This is the kind of stuff you see at the Olympics; little Laurie was in no way inferior to the best in the world! He couldn't hear anything over the friends and family around him, cheering. They were as impressed as he was.

Laurie hit her pose on sticking the dismount, then looked over at them. At *him*! Their eyes met. He was grinning ear to ear, nodding emphatically, tears in his eyes, clapping as hard as he could. A huge grin lit up her features. She flashed him the okay sign with her thumb and index finger, giving him a wink.

Erin latched onto him. When he looked at her, she was grinning, tears flowing down her cheeks. He hugged her close as Laurie paused for a breather, sipping from a water bottle.

Stef leaned over to speak to Erin. He overheard what she said, "Erin, she's been *slumming* with us!" Erin nodded agreement. Laurie's need for *personal* attention had kept her from receiving national attention, which didn't matter to her at all. She just wanted to be loved! No wonder she was so drawn to the couple. They loved her unconditionally, not for what she could do. Before today, they didn't even know what she could do!

Silence fell over the crowd as Laurie approached the balance beam. She levered up onto it, then tumbled end over end down its length, slowly. With a momentary pause, she heaved an exaggerated sigh, then backflipped to her starting point at high speed.

Gasps turned to laughter as she faced the crowd with a shocked look, doing a double take down the beam, then pointed at herself as if to say, "Did I do that?" She cartwheeled to the center, landing in a split, then put her chin on her hand like she was thinking. Shaking her head no, she raised up on her hands to swing her legs opposite of where they were. Still dissatisfied, she brought her back leg forward.

Leaning backward, she overbalanced to somersault twice in the same direction, ending up standing where she started. Facing the crowd again, she stamped her foot, looking irritated. Tumbling down the beam, she flipped back twice to the center, going even higher the second time to come down hard on both feet. It didn't stop there, though.

Jumping up and down, it looked like she intended to stomp the beam flat in a tantrum! Looking up, she noticed everyone watching. Her eyes went wide, she covered her mouth and strolled away with an innocent look, even whistling nonchalantly to the end of the beam. Chuckles came from the audience.

She began to spin in place, once, twice, three times. Leaning dizzily, she started down the beam again, a couple of steps forward, then a step back. A fall seemed inevitable as she staggered drunkenly. Slightly past the center, her feet slipped when she turned to look at the audience again. Somehow, she caught herself so her body was bent backward across the beam, balanced perfectly. Those looking on gasped again; it seemed she couldn't recover from her predicament.

Two times she tried to sit up, only to slump back unsuccessfully. Then a hand shot up with her index finger extended, like she had an idea. Crunching with abdominal muscles alone, she rose to a V position. Slowly, she brought one arm and the opposite leg to the beam together, then ratcheted her body lengthwise onto it. Applause broke out as she stood grinning, tapping her head as if to say, 'Boy, I'm smart!'

The audience loved it. Midair flips took her to the beam's end, then she flipped and tumbled its length, picking up speed to fly off the end in another elongated corkscrew spinning flip that planted her on the floor facing the end of the beam. No hint of a wobble marred her landing! The crowd cheered as she turned to face them, smiling, to take a bow. Allen shouted and clapped as hard as he could, noticing Erin was, too. They couldn't be more proud! The little titan beamed as she looked their way, then stepped off to rest.

Their section was humming with excitement, very impressed. This shared experience was bringing the company together, as new hires and old hands alike appreciated their coworker's display, discussing what they were seeing. Alissa's parents were animated, talking with each other, glancing often at the gym floor. Her little brother was staring at Laurie, even while she wasn't doing anything!

Alissa caught his eye with a thumbs up, grinning, her eyes shining. He nodded, returning the gesture with a big smile. Andrew and Carlos were visiting. The latter had his arm around his wife, who smiled when she saw him look their way. He smiled back.

Above them was another deck with more bleachers. This was the first time he paid any attention to what was behind them. He noticed someone in a wheelchair by the wall. By the clothes, he guessed it was a woman. She was bundled up as if to ward off a chill, though it wasn't cold. A scarf covered most of her features. Binoculars were in her lap. Two thoughts came to his mind: she must really want to see this, to discomfort herself, and there must be an elevator for her to get up there.

His thoughts were interrupted by Erin's touch on his arm. She directed his attention to an open area Laurie was approaching, probably designated for tumbling. Floor routines were his favorite part of gymnastics. Their girl was a born entertainer, so he really looked forward to seeing this.

When she reached one corner, she turned to zero in on the two of them. Their eyes made contact. She tapped her chest three times, then pointed right at them, nodding. Her face was utterly serious.

It touched them. Allen stood, putting his hands together to form a heart in front of his chin. She got it. Her face lit up in a happy smile. He heard noises around him, and saw her eyes open wide in surprise. The whole section was following his lead, standing to form hearts with their hands in front of them! Erin stood proudly by his side.

The gesture spread outside their section on both sides until all showed their support for the young lady on the floor, in silence. Tears glistened on her cheeks. A man's voice rang out loudly (he found out later it was Guillermo), "WE LOVE YOU, LAURIE!" Laughter broke out with applause before they all sat back down to watch.

Wiping her tears, she giggled, then spun her finger in the air. Music came on like magic, Celine Dion's *Because You Loved Me*. Allen squeezed Erin's hand as they exchanged a smile. Laurie began to dance, bringing the crowd into the melody with her, then took off on a running tumble across the floor. One big spring at the end of it somehow threw off her balance, causing her to topple and fall. A gasp went up from the crowd; his handhold with Erin went tight.

Laurie leaped back up. Unhurt, she started to resume her dance, then stopped. She waved her flat hand at her throat. The music stopped. Looking directly at Allen, she wore a rueful smile, almost a grimace as she forced a giggle. "Oops!" she said loudly. Her face was bright red, obviously embarrassed.

He couldn't help himself. Jumping up, he clapped his hands together once, then pointed at her. "YES! I TAUGHT HER THAT!" he shouted proudly.

The audience burst out laughing. Laurie doubled over, bracing her hands on her knees to keep from falling, she was laughing so hard. Whatever awkwardness she felt was forgotten, although he felt kind of weird, realizing what he had done. Turning red, he sat down, feeling foolish.

Erin spoke into his ear, "I love you!" He shrugged and gave her a cheesy grin. Laughing, she shook her head, then leaned back to his ear, "Guess we know now why you had that 'Oops' moment at the wedding, huh?" Suddenly, it made sense.

Recovering, Laurie announced loudly, "I'm gonna try that again, okay?"

Clapping broke out in a fresh show of support. She walked back to her starting corner, her eyes on Allen, laughing again. Shaking her head, she turned to ready herself, then signaled for the music. The routine was flawless this time, utterly breathtaking. On finishing, she headed toward the door she came in. Coach Radburn addressed the crowd.

"Laurie Parcille, ladies and gentlemen; her farewell performance! What do you think?"

Whistles and applause followed her to the door. When she turned, a standing ovation greeted her gaze, bringing a broad smile to her face. She waved, then exited. The Coach thanked everyone for coming out to show their support. The crowd began to disperse.

He walked over to the couple with a big smile. "That

was a delight to watch!" His hand went out to Allen, who grasped it hesitantly. Coach Radburn shook it with sincerity. "What you taught her wouldn't help her win any competitions, but as a life lesson, it's invaluable. I see why she looks up to you both." They thanked him. Turning away as others approached, he threw a wave over his shoulder, "She'll be out once she cleans up and changes."

The bulk of the spectators didn't take long to disperse. Most of their section remained, waiting for Laurie. Teresa came to them, her head shaking, "That girl is amazing!"

They agreed. The same kind of thing happened several times, as others approached with similar observations. Alissa's family was among them. Her brother asked shyly if they might meet her. The couple replied she'd be back in a few minutes if they could wait. He smiled when his folks said they would.

When Laurie came out looking fresh, spontaneous applause burst forth to greet her. A dimpled grin spread over her face. She was mobbed with hugs, and complimented over and over by those who loved her. Others came up to show their appreciation then; Carol and Tom, Alissa's family, and a few who stayed near Coach Radburn. When Hans, Alma, and Erik introduced themselves, Alissa whispered something in Dani's ear that caused her to grin.

An older man stepped forward, whom the Coach introduced as the Dean of the College. The man shook her hand warmly, stating how he enjoyed watching her. He understood from the Coach she was leaving gymnastics; he said the sport would not be as rich, without her. If she should change her mind, he had within his purview to provide a scholarship upon her enrollment. She thanked him but said she was moving to Missouri soon to be with her family. He nodded, saying he understood.

She turned to them. Erin and Allen both had tears in their eyes that came unbidden, causing her to tear up.

"Don't do that!" she told them. "It makes me cry, too!"

"Can't help it, sweetie," he hugged her tight. "We are so *proud* of you! That was incredible! Thank you so much."

Erin got her hug. "I can't believe you refused me all this time, but you did it for *him*!" she grumbled, which brought a giggle. "At least I finally got to see you strut your stuff. Laurie, you were fantastic! It was worth the wait."

"Hear, hear!" Carlos and Andrew declared together. It got them laughing, then others, too. Some clapping broke out. While they were celebrating, a middle-aged woman pushed a wheelchair into their midst. In it was the spectator with the binoculars Allen noticed earlier. A hush settled over the group, due to the interruption. The woman in the chair looked up, directly at Laurie.

Her face was impassive, her voice incredulous as she responded, *"Mother?"*

CHAPTER 18

The woman looked very thin and frail. "Hello, Laurie. I hope you don't mind that I'm here?" she seemed formal, yet humble at the same time.

Laurie was at a loss, "No... I guess not. What happened? Why are you... in that?" she pointed to the chair.

The feeble woman started to say something, then began coughing. As she covered her mouth with a tissue, the rest waited. The woman behind her placed a comforting hand on her shoulder. A bony hand covered it. The coughing passed. When she brought the tissue down, she folded it quickly, but blood was visible, for a moment. "Edna... would you... tell them?"

"Of course, Evelyn," she replied. "My name is Edna Sparks. I'm a hospice health aide. Evelyn is suffering from leukemia."

"Oh!" Laurie was stunned. She didn't see the horrified looks behind her.

Evelyn took her hand, "I didn't want to worry you, but

114

when I heard you were doing this, I couldn't stay away. Then when I saw you, my girl grown up into a young lady, I was so proud! I had to tell you, even if you sent me away."

Laurie was speechless, frozen in place. Erin was, too. If Allen read her right, she was both angry and sympathetic, waiting to see how their girl would respond. Thinking to give her time to process things, he stepped forward.

"Miss Parcille, please allow me to introduce myself. I'm Allen Edwards."

She looked at him, chuckling, "I remember, the couple who has taken the place of the parents my daughter lost... well, almost lost." Laurie looked at her, as though daring her to argue the point. Tears ran down her cheeks, "She's right, Allen. She lost us, and it's all my fault! My pride cost me the two most important people in my life while depriving her of both her parents.

"Parcille was her father's name. I went back to my maiden name, Sherwin, originally out of pride, once again. The truth is, I don't deserve to bear his name. He was only good to me. He doted on Laurie! It made me jealous. What you did when she fell a while ago is exactly the kind of thing he would have done. I couldn't have that! I was building a champion; I needed perfection from her. In the end, I drove her away, too."

She turned back to Laurie, "It wasn't fair, what I demanded from you. You forfeited your childhood for my ambition. My mortality has caused me to review my life. I understand now I have been a blight on the people I care about most! Not a day goes by I don't regret it. I don't blame you if you can't forgive me, but I hope you will."

"Mother," Laurie heaved a deep breath, "I don't know if I can. Even having accepted Jesus, who is all about forgiveness, I just don't know. I need time to think and pray."

Evelyn grasped her hand again lightly, "However much

time I have is yours, my girl. That's not exactly fair, but it's the best I have to offer. If I don't see you again, then I'll know your decision has been made. In that case, I want you to know it's been *wonderful* seeing you again. I love you, Laurie! It was stupid pride that kept me from telling you before."

She said goodbye, then her aide pushed her toward the door. Laurie watched partway, then suddenly buried her head into Allen's shoulder, sobbing. He put his arms around her and let her cry.

Alissa asked, "What is hospice?"

Her mother answered, "It's what healthcare for the terminally ill is called, sweetheart."

Hans added sadly, "It's only provided if you have less than six months to live."

Not knowing what else to do, Allen called them all to pray for Laurie and her mother. Hans and Alma might not be religious, but under the circumstances, they bowed their heads respectfully. Their eyes widened when, after a moment, their daughter stepped forward to join the prayer group with a glance toward them. Erik watched her curiously, casting sympathetic looks toward Laurie. Peace settled over them immediately. Laurie's sobs dried up. The prayer only lasted a minute or so.

Laurie released him but stayed very close. She managed a smile, "Thanks, everyone. That helps a lot, along with knowing you care about me. I'm gonna have to forgive her, aren't I, Dad?"

Allen shrugged, and gave her a half-smile, "Honey, it's the only way you'll ever have peace. Besides, Jesus forgave you, set that example. You follow Him now. How can you do any less than He did for you?"

"I don't know how much I'll mean it. There's so much history there!"

"My girl, *you* choose your course when you know what's right, and the feelings will follow. Not everything in you is anger toward her. Some of it is hurt. When you forgive, the anger begins to subside, so the Lord can start healing the hurt. It's not about whether she deserves your forgiveness, it's about being made whole before Him. He wants that for you. It's why He brought her here."

"*Jesus* brought her here? You think so?" That surprised her.

"Like a moth to a bright light, yes. You heard her say she couldn't stay away."

Dani spoke, "Everything about today has been about bringing closure to your past, sis. You couldn't get that without resolving the issues with your mother, you know?"

Laurie heaved a sigh, "No, I guess not. Well, maybe some good will come of it."

Allen put his arm around Erin, drawing her close with a grin she returned, "When I led Erin to Christ, she became my treasure in heaven. You are, too! Everyone you lead to salvation becomes your treasure in heaven. How would you like to stand before Jesus, knowing part of the treasure laid up for you in eternity is your mother?"

She was floored, "*That* could happen? Really?"

He shrugged again, "It's up to her, but stranger things have happened. Nothing is too difficult for God."

Hans inquired, "Then why doesn't He heal her?" There was dead silence. "He does that kind of thing, I've heard it claimed, so why not for her?"

"He could," Allen replied evenly, "but I don't know if He will. Just like we have the choice whether to believe God's word for salvation in Christ Jesus, He also chooses what He will or will not do. Unless He has committed Himself to a promise, we have no way of knowing what He will choose. One of those choices He reserves for Himself is how long we live on this Earth.

"That is a matter of the highest importance from the human perspective, Hans, but what about from an eternal perspective? If she doesn't have her eternity laid out, what difference does it make whether she lives six months or twenty years? The end is still the same."

"So He doesn't value human life, then."

"Oh, yes, He does! He created it, so of course He values it, but not for the same reasons we do. We go about it like it's all there is, so it's all that matters. He sees it as the grace period to choose our eternal destination. He has declared that He will *raise all the dead* for eternal existence in the destination of our choice, heaven or hell.

"Those who refuse to believe His declaration now choose by default. When they *are* raised, they'll realize how badly they were mistaken, but the time to repent will be past. What nation willingly tolerates rebels in its borders? God will expel all who rebel against Him, too, even angels."

"I guess that makes sense, Allen. I see why our daughter bought into it, but I don't like it."

"I understand, but the alternative is that when we die, we are nothing more than food for the worms. If that's the case, where did our sense of right and wrong originate? Animals don't display it, but justice is *very* important to us; whether we do good or evil in our lives, the grave awaits us all."

"Is that just? However, if we inherited this trait from our Creator, who formed us in His likeness, then it's no mystery. Furthermore, it is a comfort to know no injustice will be overlooked when God will judge the living and the dead."

"The foremost injustice is that God made His Word flesh to be sacrificed for our sins, yet we loved them more than we loved Him. Every other injustice pales in comparison! It is the heart of the eternal rebel. God will expel that person from His kingdom, but just like you, He won't like it. He would rather welcome us as the family of Christ."

"Alissa has obtained something wonderful from her

Heavenly Father that cannot be taken from her. Her Earthly father would be wise to look into it. Over this week we are in town, God will prove Himself to you and Alma three times to let you know He is real, beyond any shadow of a doubt. If you receive Him, your family will be saved from sin, assured of a place in heaven. If you reject Him, you will become His enemy and *lose everything that matters to you.* I get that you are a no-nonsense man. You are about to meet a God who will brook no nonsense, as well. Don't test Him!"

His mouth clapped shut, a look of outrage on his face. He *growled*, then turned on his heel, grabbed his wife by the arm, and stalked off with the kids in tow.

"You know he won't let Alissa visit us now," Teresa observed with regret.

He shook his head with a little smile, "Give it a week, sister. The Lord's working on him. He's not about to abandon Alissa! That youngster stood up for Him when she chose to pray with us. There's *no way* He'll do any less for her! We'll uphold her in prayer. When she returns to us, she'll have a new testimony to share!" That got several smiles.

CHAPTER 19

Hans was beside himself with fury. How dare that man speak to him that way! He was a civil engineer with more accolades than that Missouri bumpkin could dream of. Governments had consulted him before undertaking projects involving many millions of dollars! This man had the gall to lecture him about God, as though He is real?

He and his wife had always been too intelligent to accept superstitious drivel of a being whose existence couldn't be empirically proven. If mankind couldn't prove God is real, the idea wasn't worth further time or thought. Now Allen says God will *finally* prove Himself real? Let Him!

It bothered him that his daughter had been taken in, though. Their children inherited their intelligence. He never thought Alissa would fall for such nonsense. Allen read him right about that. He had little patience for foolishness. What had she been told, to cause her to accept their beliefs? They had been exposed to religious people before, both kids, but never shown an interest in taking their beliefs to heart. What was different this time?

Alma visited with the kids, giving him space to cool down. They discussed Laurie's display, which impressed them all. Alissa had convinced her parents she would be worth seeing. It turned out to be an understatement. Laurie Parcille was Olympic material, no question.

The young lady had a full plate, being estranged from her mother, then learning she was dying. Hans hated death! Too many people he cared about had succumbed to it, over his lifetime. Death should always be deferred as long as possible, the way it cut short human potential and caused grief. Allen's attitude seemed callous to him.

Having cooled off, he wanted to talk to Alissa and hear how she had been taken in. It should be a family discussion. He and Alma decided long ago that open discussion was the right way to raise the kids to be rational and open-minded. He broke his silence to propose stopping for ice cream cones. Of course, the idea was well-received. It also let the family know he was approachable again. That was intentional, too. Hans and his wife were very intentional people.

Once they had treats in hand, they settled at a table. He knew Alma was as curious as he was about their daughter's newly acquired beliefs, but would wait for him to take the lead to investigate. Now he did so.

"So, Alissa," he opened the conversation, "you joined in prayer for that gymnast and her ailing mother today." She nodded, waiting. "How long have you held to their beliefs?"

"It's been a little over two months, ever since I played at the wedding, Daddy. That was the first time I met them."

He remembered, nodding. "Your mother and I know you are very intelligent, not easily deceived. *You* know that we do not believe as they do, else you would not have hidden your new persuasion from us. We're not angry, just disappointed you thought that was necessary."

She swallowed nervously, but showed no signs of shame. He felt a little proud of her, for that! "Allen said I should look into this, so I am taking his advice. What did they say to convince you to accept their beliefs for your own, sweetheart?" Reminding her that Allen recommended he be curious was a good call. She seemed to relax.

She leaned forward, taking them into her confidence, "Actually, it was less about what they said, more about what I saw, then *felt*. I played the wedding march as planned, then Allen prayed, but not like any prayer I've ever heard. He invited God to the wedding, *and He came!* A wind like a hurricane shook the trees, yet never touched the ground, just for a few seconds. When it stopped, it was totally quiet. Something was there, invisible but undeniable, that made everyone want to not make a sound!"

"It wasn't *bad*. I don't know exactly how to describe it. It seemed peaceful, even happy to be there. Allen said something that made people laugh, and it was okay to move again, even though that *presence* was still there. It stayed throughout the ceremony; I'm not sure when it left. I *knew* God was real when that happened. No one had to tell me anything to convince me.

"I didn't know what to do about it, though. Did you notice that really tall man at the gym, Andrew?" They chuckled, nodding. He was impossible to miss! "Right after the wedding, he asked Jesus into his heart. It made me think. We went in to have cake, then people started leaving. It got down to a dozen or so, the same people that hung around the gym with Allen and Erin after everyone else left.

"The Mexican family I pointed out a while ago… remember?" They did. "Juanita and Carlos were the ones that got married. They were already Christians. Reina and Guillermo, his mother and brother, were Catholic, like Teresa. They had questions to ask Allen, and Teresa said she did, too. He answered everything they asked, telling them how Jesus died for people's sins on the cross, then came back to life to justify their faith in Him. I've heard it before, but this time it made *sense* like never before.

"I still didn't do anything about it, but Guillermo asked something that brought a surprising answer from Allen. Guillermo was *gay,* Daddy. He told us later that he had been since the ninth grade. Allen said *demons* cause that!"

Hans sat back, folding his arms across his chest. Alma shook her head, her lips pursed. Their body language made it clear how intolerant they considered that statement. Erik continued to listen, since his sister was plainly not finished.

She also sat back, but she didn't stop. "Allen looked at me, interrupting himself to warn me that he was going to talk about demons. He said if it made me uncomfortable, it might be better for me to leave the room, but he didn't make me. I asked to stay; somehow, I felt like I needed to be there. I am so glad I stayed!

"After he told us how they work, Guillermo asked him to cast the demon out of him. Allen did, and like *four* of them came out! I have *never* heard four voices coming out of one person, all at the same time, until then. He asked Jesus to forgive him and come into his heart at that point. His mother Reina, Teresa, and I did the same, we were so moved. It changed all of us, on the inside. I can't describe it! We're all different, like something that was missing is there now."

Her mother checked, "Is Guillermo still gay?"

Alissa shook her head emphatically, "No, Mama. He said he isn't interested in guys anymore."

Hans took a deep breath, "Well, I have to admit, if I experienced what you described, it would make me rethink things, too. Until we are sure you are safe with these people, you won't be going to see them. We can't risk them turning out to be some dangerous cult! If you keep a good attitude and don't hide anything else from us, you can keep your cell phone, for now."

He anticipated anger or outrage, but that wasn't her response. She *smiled*, "Okay, Daddy."

"Okay?" he was stunned.

She nodded. "God promised to prove Himself to you this week. I can wait that long!"

CHAPTER 20

A number of their group had things to do after the exhibition, so they made plans to meet for dinner that evening. Laurie decided to go see her mother. Allen was very proud of her and told her so. Dani went to see her father, too, hoping he would recognize her. It was draining, she said, so she was looking forward to time with them afterward. They told both young ladies they were there for them.

They asked Emily if she was busy. She wasn't and was pleased to hear they wanted to visit with her. The three of them met back at the house to discuss her move. It turned out she had been putting money back for some time, so she had something to fall back on in case something bad happened. A friend planned to buy her car, which she would then replace in Missouri. No furnishings she owned were worth transporting, so she was gifting or selling it all. She anticipated starting fresh in Missouri.

Allen wondered, didn't she have anything of sentimental value to her? Two things, she said: a locket she was wearing, given to her by her mother, and the Bible he gave her! Those will be going with her on the plane, she announced with a grin. Everything else but clothes was replaceable. No one could accuse her of being materialistic, he thought to himself! To her delight, Erin booked her flight with them on the spot. They visited up until they left for dinner.

Dani returned in time to ride with them. Her father had mistaken her for her mother. The visit was awkward; she left when he became amorous! Emily offered to go with her next time. Erin said it might be a good idea to take someone with her from now on. They all wondered how Laurie's visit was going.

She arrived at the restaurant minutes after they were seated, quieter than usual, and settled beside Allen. He wrapped an arm around her shoulders, pulling her up against him. She leaned her head on his shoulder.

"You want to talk now, or later?" he asked in a low tone.

"Later, I think," she whispered. He nodded.

The rest picked up on her dampened demeanor, responding by joking and silliness that did have an effect. She brightened; the usual joy began to assert its place in her, as the evening progressed. When Reina inquired if Allen was going to teach her how to yawn, his feigned outrage got a big belly laugh from Laurie, followed by lots of giggles. Obviously, Guillermo came by his orneriness honestly, he noted. Smiling, Reina shrugged. Gui nodded emphatically. They prayed for Alissa before going their separate ways.

Emily and Dani rode with the couple and Laurie met them at the house. Stef was there, so all settled to visit together, as Laurie clued them in.

"Mother is different now. I've never seen her weak like this. She said chemo is what caused her to start coughing up blood. She's been through two rounds of it, but it hasn't helped. *She's dying!* I was *so* angry with her, but... I never wished this on her. It kind of feels like it's my fault, 'cause I left."

Heads shook all around her. "No way is this your fault, girl," Stef replied sympathetically. "Things like this happen, sometimes. It's nobody's fault, not even hers. Don't take that on yourself."

"You are here for her now, Laurie. She drew comfort from your presence, just in the brief moments she saw you at the gym," Erin pointed out.

"Yeah, that's why I stayed with her as long as I did. I saw that. Edna thanked me for coming, said it perked her up. I told her I forgave her, Dad. She *cried*! She never used to cry, but she did about that. I have to admit, it was like a load lifted off of me, too. Is that what you meant?"

"It is. Someone said holding a grudge is like drinking poison, then expecting the one you're angry with to die. It only hurts the one it embitters. When Jesus forgave you, even though you didn't deserve it, you received grace to do the same for others. He has liberated you, so you can."

She nodded, "I didn't know that, before today."

Turning to Stefanie, she added slowly, "Stef, I'm not ready to give notice, not yet. I guess I want to stand by my mother, while she fights for her life. Part of me can't believe what I'm saying, but…"

"I got you, sweetheart. You're making a wise decision, in my opinion. Life is lived best without regrets. Make the guys who are dumb enough to challenge you bear all the regrets!" That brought laughter from all of them, especially Laurie.

"At least she didn't make a pass at you!" Emily declared. Blank scowls appeared on Stef and Laurie. It prompted Dani to tell them about her visit with her father, how he thought she was her mother and tried to become intimate! Stef chuckled, then immediately apologized.

Laurie was shocked! She expressed sympathy. Dani reassured her she knew it wasn't deliberate. He thought it was his wife before him. His mind was playing tricks on him, both in mistaking her identity and forgetting his wife passed away years ago.

She admitted it *did* make things awkward, though. Emily said she planned to go with her, next time. Stef and Laurie volunteered to go along on future visits.

"I admire your generous heart, Emily, but how do expect to go with her if you're in Missouri?" Stef inquired practically.

Emily colored, "I-I didn't think of that. Sorry, Dani."

She grinned, "Don't worry about it. You meant well. These two are willing to help me with this, and I suspect Juanita will be, too. Being pregnant has put her out of work, so she will probably be bored at home. This would get her out of the house."

Allen thought that was good thinking. Something else occurred to him. "Dani, do you have any pictures of your mother?"

Smiling, she reached into her purse, "Yes, I do. We were really close. It hit me hard when she got sick, but she suffered so much with the cancer, I was relieved when her pain ended. We all missed her, though." Flipping open a collection of wallet photos, she found the one she wanted, then handed them over. He and Erin let out a gasp. Danielle was almost a ringer for her mom!

"*No wonder* he thought you were her!" Erin exclaimed. "You look just like her!" They passed it around, so everyone could see.

"You think so?" Dani was flattered. "I always thought Mom was so pretty!" Heads were shaking, amazed at the resemblance.

"Well, now we know where you get it from," Stef observed. "In about ten more years, you could be her twin. That's crazy!" she grinned.

Allen laughed, "Don't take any guys with you to see him, sis. If he thinks you're his wife with another man, he's liable to clobber him!"

Her jaw dropped, "I hadn't thought of that. It never crossed my mind a visit could get even *more* awkward than it did today!" The thought cracked them up, even Dani!

CHAPTER 21

Alissa was texting back and forth with a friend after dinner, lying on her bed, when a knock on her door disturbed her. She invited whoever it was to come in. It turned out to be her brother. Erik could be a brat at times, but not as much as he used to be. Middle school had brought about changes in him, or perhaps it was puberty. Whatever it was, he seemed to value his big sister as a sounding board more often now. It had drawn them closer together, a welcome change from his taking pleasure in annoying her.

"Hey, can we talk?" he wondered.

"Sure, I guess," she put down her phone, sitting up.

He sat at her desk, spinning the chair to face her. "That stuff you told us today... That was pretty intense. You didn't make that up, did you?" It was more a statement than a question. His expression was earnest, not at all mocking.

"You know I don't do things like that."

"Yeah, I know. I didn't think you'd lie. It's not easy to trick you, either; *believe me*, I know!" he grinned. She smiled back.

He became serious again. "I *really* like Laurie. She's amazing! When her mother left and Laurie cried, I wanted to help. I couldn't stand to see it, but there was nothing I could do. You stepped forward to pray for her with those people, though. That was pretty cool, you know."

"Well, thank you," she replied, surprised. She knew he had a crush on Laurie; she even whispered her observation into Dani's ear, making her smile. She had to tell someone, but she never intended to embarrass him, so she told her friends. Since they didn't know her brother, there was no risk of shaming him.

"It sucks when you see someone hurting, but there's nothing you can do to help," he noted. She nodded. "I could ask God to help if I knew He was real. Since you're convinced He is, is there a way I can know for sure, too?"

Tears streaked down her cheeks, unbidden. He looked concerned, worried he said something wrong. She giggled, reached for a tissue, "Sorry, it's a girl thing." He grinned, nodding.

"Erik, believing is a *choice*. You don't believe *because* you know; you believe, and then you know. That's why it's called faith. I saw stuff I couldn't explain that caused me to believe in Jesus. It moved me to pray to Him by faith, confessing He is real and alive, asking Him to forgive me for my sins. When He came into my heart, that's when I *knew* He is real. Without taking a leap of faith, *no one* can know for sure."

He shook his head slowly, "I might be able to do that, but Mom and Dad won't have anything to do with Jesus if they can't prove He is real, first."

Her grin was ear to ear, "They won't have to. God is going to prove Himself to them *this week*, according to what Allen told Dad. Nothing I have heard Allen say about God has turned out to be wrong, yet. It's gonna be fun to see what God does for them!"

He nodded, thinking, "Okay. Laurie believes in Jesus too, she said. Can you tell me about Him?" She did. Opening her Bible, the two of them began reading together, talking over what they discovered. Though Erik made no decision that evening, he was absorbed as they delved into scripture, also enjoying time with his sister. The Holy Spirit taught them as they studied together.

The next morning, Hans was frustrated by fog on his way to work. It made for poor visibility, not to mention unpredictable behavior from other drivers on the road. Some were barely moving, while others let haste overcome caution to become hazards for everyone else. Being Monday morning, traffic was thick, making his patience thin.

All of it combined created a recipe for disaster. Hans maneuvered his little two-seat sports car onto the freeway carefully, hoping to make up some time. The car was his baby. He refused to give it up, no matter how impractical it was for the family. Alma had given up trying to persuade him. He could be immovable when he set his mind on something, like holding onto his toy. Fortunately, he didn't often take that kind of stand.

Finding a gap in traffic, he managed 35 mph for a short while. Feeling good about his progress, he rounded a curve to come upon a pile-up directly in front of him! A tractor-trailer was on its side blocking the road, along with at least half a dozen vehicles that had smashed into it. No emergency services were on the scene, so it must have just happened. Hans stomped the brakes. On the wet road, there was no way he could stop in time!

Out of the corner of his eye, he thought he saw a glowing white figure in the passenger seat. He almost looked as the car skidded forward toward impact, but an air horn drew his attention to his side mirror, instead. Another rig was coming up on him fast from behind! Just like that,

Hans realized his death was imminent.

What happened next was never quite clear. Gripping the wheel so tightly his knuckles turned white, he clenched his teeth and ducked his head. A loud screeching sound made his eyes clench shut involuntarily. Miraculously the car came to a stop without any impacts in front or behind. His eyes opened cautiously. The car was stopped on the freeway with no other vehicles close.

A glance in the mirrors caused him to spin around in his seat. The pile-up was perhaps ten feet behind him! He had somehow *passed through* it. It was impossible; the road was completely blocked! He heard the sound of more collisions, then saw the rig on its side being thrust closer to him. In near panic, he stepped on the gas to put distance between them.

He didn't stop until he got to work. When he got out, his knees wobbled. Along the driver's side, a deep groove scarred the length of the car. Death had been inches from him! He was rattled to the core as he went in and settled at his desk. For a few minutes, he just sat there, *breathing*. It was like reassurance, what he had taken for granted all his life.

His intercom buzzed. The Vice President wanted to see him in his office. Rising cautiously, he made sure his knees would hold him, then made his way to the destination. The VP greeted him cheerfully and offered him a seat. As he bent down to sit, he froze. The boss had a calendar on his desk with a daily scripture quote. Hans noticed it many times before. Accomplished at reading things upside down, he had developed a habit of reading the quotes. In a way, he thought of it like reading a fortune cookie.

The current quote restarted his jitters. It read:
"Whosoever shall seek to save his life will lose it;
and whosoever shall lose his life shall preserve it."
Luke 17:33
For Hans, it read like an ultimatum from God: either

give me your life, or it will be *taken* from you! In light of his brush with death, it came across deadly serious.

His boss, Ted, asked if something was wrong. He shook a little as he sat, then told him he had been in an accident coming to work. Ted was concerned, sympathetic, even took a look at his car. Upon close inspection, he concluded Hans must have been sideswiped. When his employee couldn't account for what happened, he told him to take the day off to collect himself, and maybe get checked out. Hans thanked him, then carefully made his way home.

Alma was very surprised to see him. He told her everything; that's the kind of relationship they had. She cried when she saw the damage, so close to the driver, saying she *knew* the car was a death trap. That's why she asked him to get rid of it!

After recovering her composure in his arms, she turned on the news. The pile-up was prominently covered. Forty-nine vehicles were involved. Emergency services were everywhere. The death toll was at sixteen, so far, but rescue efforts were not complete. It was a mangled mess! The estimated time to clean it up was at least three days.

Turning off the TV, she pinned him with her gaze. "You said when you saw it, there was a semi and six or seven cars blocking the road?"

He nodded, "Yes."

"*You* should be dead, buried beneath all those vehicles that came up behind you. I despise your Miata, but no car could have protected you from that, I have to admit."

Subdued, he agreed. He knew the semi overtaking him in his mirror should have been the end of him! "I don't know how I got past it like I did."

"There's only one explanation, *mein herr*; that glowing figure in your passenger seat. Nothing else makes sense. When all possibilities are ruled out, the impossible must be considered." His expression was as though he had just bit into a lemon. "I don't like it, either, but it's where logic takes us. I prefer it over burying you, then raising the kids myself!"

"I don't blame you, *liebchen*. I wouldn't want to face life without you. But if angels are real, then God is real, and the world is not the way we thought it was. Even God is different! He *isn't* love incarnate if He's threatening my life. He can't be!"

The discussion continued until it was nearly time for the children to return from school. They agreed what happened should remain between them, rather than worry the kids. Picking Alissa's brain for information about God repulsed them, too. There was no way to do it without the appearance they were attacking her beliefs. It wouldn't be fair to her; moreover, they didn't want to lose her trust.

Needing information, they were at an impasse. Like a cow chewing its cud, they kept regurgitating what they did know, which was insufficient to draw any conclusions. Little by little, Allen's words from the day before began to assimilate into their thinking. He said if Hans rejected Christ, he would become His enemy and all he valued would be taken from him.

It was infuriating to hear at the time, but it did align with the scripture he read on Ted's desk. If his life was taken from him, nothing else *would* matter to him, would it? Hans hated death, but everyone dies, sooner or later. Six months or twenty years; what *real* difference does it make, if the outcome is unchanged? Can it be changed?

Perhaps God *isn't* threatening his life. If he sees mortality as the grace period for deciding an eternal destination, and there's no guarantee how long one's life is anyway, then why *couldn't* He choose to condense the time to make that decision down to a single week? If not for the miracle of surviving this morning, Hans' time would already be up. If anything, God wasn't cheating him out of life, He *extended it!*

All this was thought through and discussed throughout

the evening, and into the next day. A newscast declared the final mortality count of the pile-up at nineteen, though several of those hospitalized were in critical condition. Calling that count 'final' might be premature. If God were his enemy, he would have been in that number, he decided.

CHAPTER 22

On the way home Tuesday, he verbalized to no one there, "If You're there and You're real, *why* did You protect me?" The thought came instantly to mind, "My girl is praying for you." *My girl is praying for me*, he thought. It made him smile, then it hit him; that's not what he thought. *My* girl is praying for *you*. It wasn't *his* thought, it was the answer to his question!

Allen had differentiated that his daughter had a heavenly Father while acknowledging himself as her earthly father. He, Hans, would not tolerate *anyone* coming between him and his kids, not for one minute! Could an invisible God stake a claim on a human life, then be jealous if that claim was not recognized? A chill ran down his spine as he considered it.

Over dinner that night, he asked Alissa if she was praying for her family. Alma was surprised but looked at her daughter.

"Well, of course, Daddy," she replied brightly. "I love you guys."

"Good. We love you, too," he reassured her. "May I ask what you request when you pray, or is that too personal?"

She hesitated, coloring a bit. "No, it's not too personal, but it might make you angry. I asked Jesus to save you all, like He did for me. My friends are praying for you too, because I asked them to. I hope it's okay?"

He couldn't help but smile. "Why wouldn't it be? You only mean good for us, right?" She nodded enthusiastically. Erik smiled, as did Alma. They were a close family. Hans was proud of that. "I have some questions I am thinking of asking Allen, honey. Would you give me his number? Do you think he would talk to me?"

Her grin threatened to split her face, "Daddy, the answer to both questions is - gladly." She read it off, while he entered it into his contacts. "I know he made you angry, but it wasn't intentional. He's just blunt, sometimes, when he's making his point. He doesn't beat around the bush. He's a lot like you, that way."

Alma grinned. She had pointed out that tendency in him many times over the years. He smiled, "Do you think that's a good quality?"

Both kids nodded. "Yes, I do. It makes what you say easy to understand, and makes you both good teachers."

He thanked her. It's satisfying to hear your child admires you. Alissa wasn't so much a child anymore, so her assessments were mature enough to deserve some respect. Even her brother realized that, now. It showed in how he treated her. His heart swelled with pride for his family.

He wondered, if God was real, did He ever feel this way? "*My girl* is praying for you." Upon remembrance, that *did* sound proud of her. Prayer definitely wasn't part of his way of thinking, either. If only the whole subject of God wasn't so foreign to him!

One thing was clear: his daughter asked for God to save him, and yesterday morning *something* certainly did. It seemed her request was taken literally. The deep scratch on his car left no doubt that was real.

Alma inquired privately if he was seriously considering calling Allen. He admitted he was, then told her of his question spoken aloud in his car, followed by what seemed to be a response. He confirmed it was true by talking to Alissa.

"I am out of my depth, dear one. Who should I confer with? I don't trust religious people, yet that is the realm of my confusion. Alissa does trust Allen, so maybe I can. Besides, it would be good to know more about him, to make certain he is no danger to her. What do you think?"

She smiled, "I'm glad for your choice, if you can control your temper." He smiled sheepishly. "If God *is* real, we don't want Him as our enemy."

The next day, after kicking the idea around, he finally tried to call Allen. The call did not go through, for some reason. There wasn't time to try again. Company business took him to the Planning Commission in the county courthouse. As he headed to the elevators on his way out afterward, it seemed he spied a glowing figure in white on his right side; but when he looked, no one was there.

The sound of an elevator door got his attention. Someone got out, leaving it empty, so he started sprinting to catch it before it closed. The next moment, he was on the floor, his nose bleeding from the impact. He had tripped! More embarrassed than hurt, he retreated to the restroom to quell the bleeding. It did stop, though it was swelling noticeably. Feeling foolish, he caught another elevator and rode it down.

When he got out, a crowd of onlookers nearly blocked his path. His eye followed their attention to one side, where maintenance and security staff struggled to open the doors of another elevator. As he watched, they succeeded, revealing a *crushed* car that was thankfully empty. The crowd heaved a sigh of relief, but Hans was chilled to the bone, realizing it was the elevator his fall prevented him from reaching!

Shaken, he took a seat in the lobby to give his nerves time to settle. Was someone trying to kill him? It made no sense, he decided. He remembered the glowing figure he thought he saw, just before he fell. *That fall saved his life!* If the figure tripped him, he owed it a debt of gratitude.

Again, he tried calling Allen with no luck. His daughter's prayers came back to mind. The thought brought some comfort. The quivering inside him subsided enough to stand and get moving again. Having planned his errand late in the workday, there was no need to return to the job until tomorrow, so he headed home.

Mortality weighed heavily on him from the week's events. His swollen nose was certain to raise questions, especially from his family. He was getting scared, truthfully. It was becoming difficult to shield them from worry, with fear creeping into his own heart. When he arrived home, he called for Alissa first thing, even before greeting his spouse.

Both kids answered his call; apparently, they were together. Alma came to see what was up from the kitchen. This wasn't how he normally behaved on arriving home. All expressed concern at his swollen nose. A little embarrassed, he told them he fell. They were not satisfied, but he changed the subject. It didn't stall them for long.

"I've been trying to reach Allen, but the calls aren't getting through," he told his daughter. "Do you think he's angry with me?" *That didn't come out like I wanted*, he chided himself.

Phone in hand, she was tapping away, "Nuh-uh, I doubt it. Hang on, I'm texting Laurie to see where he is." Erik lit up at the mention of the gymnast's name.

"How did you fall?" his wife pressed.

"Down… on my nose," he joked. She was not amused. She knew him too well and could tell there was something off with him. Starting to say something, she stopped as Alissa got a response.

"Daddy, Laurie says he and Erin are out of town. They went to see the giant trees at Sequoia National Park, a ways from Fresno. She isn't sure if they get a signal out there. They'll return Friday."

Well, that made sense, he thought. Three sets of eyes watched him expectantly. He knew he'd tell Alma everything before the night was out. When he looked at Alissa, he came to an unexpected conclusion. If he was taking comfort in the knowledge she was praying for him, she deserved to know it! He promised to tell them everything over the dinner table. Alma raised an eyebrow at his decision, but left it at that and returned to the kitchen. They went to wash up.

At dinner, he kept his promise. Starting with the close call at the elevator, because his partner didn't know of it yet, he then recounted what happened on the freeway Monday morning. Shock blanketed all three of their faces! His gaze settled on his daughter, hoping what had been some comfort to him might help quell their fear.

"Neither of these disasters was supernatural. They could happen to anyone, at any time. The supernatural part is *that I survived*! I don't know if I believe in God, but the glowing white figure I saw each time indicates someone is protecting me when I can't protect myself. The only explanation I can find is that your prayers are being answered, little one. You asked for us to be saved, and twice now, I have been! Thank you for praying. Please don't stop!"

In tears, Alissa nodded. "You won't die, Daddy, not this week. Jesus is proving Himself, just like Allen said He would. You have to live for that to happen!"

"You may be right. Before the events of this week, I would not have admitted that. My perspective is changing, with all that has happened."

It worked. Alissa's reassurance seemed to give them all something to hold onto. There was *hope*, a point to all this that would surface shortly. Upon finishing their meal, the kids went to the garage to see the gouge on his car, then returned shaking their heads. Dad would usually be fuming over damage to his car, more proof he was just happy to be alive.

When they were alone, Alma thanked him for sharing with the kids. Unsure if it was wise at first, it helped knowing she wasn't alone with her worry anymore. He told her the family was strongest when they stood together. She concurred.

CHAPTER 23

Thursday morning, Hans once again stood before the company VP. Once again, he read the calendar on the desk as he sat down. It stated:

"Lo, children are an heritage of the Lord: and the fruit of the womb is his
reward." Psalm 127:3

He hesitated, then asked his boss what he thought it meant.

Ted was very surprised. "I didn't know you had an interest in Biblical things, Hans." He sat back as he thought, "Well, I'm not a minister or a Bible teacher, just a sinning schmuck Jesus saved in His mercy, so I can't give you a definitive answer. All I can tell you is what it means to me, okay?

"People sometimes say children are a gift from God. You've probably heard that." Hans nodded. "Well, I don't think it's completely accurate. We both have kids. We both love 'em, too, but I think they are more of a *trust* God delivers into our care, rather than a gift. Just because he gives them to us, doesn't mean He gives up His claim to them. They are ours, yet they are still *His*, too. If we don't raise them in the fear and admonition of God, He will hold us responsible for our failure."

What Allen said, that Alissa had a heavenly Father *and* an earthly father, returned to mind. Ted was making sense. He thanked him for the explanation. An odd smile was on the man's face. He reached over to open a desk drawer, then pulled out a box and handed it across to Hans. In it was a nice new leather-bound Bible!

"That's for you. I purchased it a few weeks ago for you, felt like I should, but I chickened out about giving it to you because I didn't want to offend. Didn't want you to think I was insulting your intelligence!"

It dismayed Hans to think Ted would hesitate to approach him. Did he come across so narrow-minded? He admired his boss too much to brush aside anything he said. Thanking him, he came to a decision. Hans laid out everything he had experienced since the exhibition Sunday afternoon. Ted's eyebrows climbed so high up his forehead, it looked like they might merge with his hair!

"Dear Lord, Hans!" he burst out when the tale was finished. "No wonder you were so rattled Monday! I don't know what to say. How are you not a basket case of nerves, by now?"

With a wry smile, Hans replied, "I'm not exactly sure. My daughter and her friends are praying for me to Jesus. I'm not sure He's real, but they believe He is. The way this glowing figure keeps popping in to prevent my death has me wondering. If he wanted me dead, I'd *be* dead! All he'd have to do is stand back and watch, stay out of it. He isn't threatening me, he's saving me from what would have happened naturally, otherwise."

Ted grinned, shaking his head. "I never would have thought of it that way. Do you realize how unusual your take on this is? Most folks, me included, would think of this as God threatening your life to get what He wants from you, which *doesn't* fit with how scripture presents Him. It would scare us away from Him!

"You're right, though, in your outlook. You are seeing things more clearly than I am. This fellow Allen is supposed to be back tomorrow?" He nodded. "If I were you, Hans, I'd go see him. This is too vital to handle with a phone call." That made sense. "Could I go with you?"

The request took him by surprise. "If I go, I guess so. May I ask why? You already believe in Christ, don't you?"

Ted nodded, "I do, but... I've never seen Him work like this, never even heard of it. This is outside my experience. God is *doing* things I'd like to see, if you'll let me tag along or meet you there."

Hans was gracious, "I'll let you know if we go see him; you're welcome if we do. I have to call him first, even if it's just to set it up. Fair enough?"

Ted shook his hand, thanking him. He was excited! It puzzled Hans as their attention turned back to work. Why would someone like his boss consider Allen's group extraordinary? Was there something different about them than what he had in church?

His daughter seemed to think so. No church had ever moved her, so maybe there was. No "man of God" ever got under his skin like Allen had, so *that* was different for him, he thought wryly. Perhaps God is annoying too, if He's real! It would be hard to hold that against Him, if it turns out *He's* the One who's been saving his life.

CHAPTER 24

On Monday and Tuesday, Erin and Allen felt like their presence in California served no real purpose. With everyone working, there wasn't much interaction with them. It was awkward, taking up Stef's quarters, even though she said nothing to cause that feeling. She seemed to enjoy having them around. Laurie's visits with her mother were a little tense for her at first, so she drew comfort from their presence, but didn't *really* need them.

Tuesday morning, Reina and Juanita came to visit and they went to lunch together. While out, Allen and Erin expressed how they felt like they were taking up space at the house needlessly, yet the Lord had indicated they should remain in California for the week. Reina suggested the couple take a day or two to go sightseeing. The idea intrigued them! Allen had not seen redwoods since he was little. Erin was all for it, so they prayed, then left Wednesday morning.

They had a blast! Just the two of them traveling together, so intimate and relaxed. They enjoyed the road, two nights in a cabin, and the biggest trees on earth! Erin was awestruck. These were even larger than those he saw as a kid. They were out of touch Thursday, so the conference call went undone, but the time alone admiring God's handiwork was unique and precious in its own right. They headed back on Friday refreshed, ready to see what He would do with them next.

As they drew closer to urban areas, he received a call from Hans! No longer angry, he asked to meet with them sometime on Saturday. Sure, Allen replied, but they probably wouldn't be alone. Would that be okay? He laughed. He was bringing the family and his boss, he said! He assured him there was nothing private about this. They set a time to meet at the house. Erin put plans in motion to grill and invited his boss's family, too! Hans was delighted at their hospitality and said he'd pass along the invitation.

"The Lord certainly changed his attitude," Erin observed with a smile. She had been texting nonstop, putting plans together. "I wonder what we missed."

He rested his hand on her thigh. "Whatever happened, we'll catch up tomorrow. Being with you was the best place in the world for me, Genie, wherever we were. I didn't miss anything; that's the truth!" She lifted his hand, kissed the back of it, then replaced it on her thigh and covered it with her own as she grinned at him. It put a smile on his face for the rest of the drive!

Arriving at the house around mid-afternoon, it was busy enough in the studio their entrance seemed to go unnoticed. Security cameras picked them up, though, Erin assured him. Sure enough, Dani came out to greet them, followed moments later by Laurie. Soaked with sweat in a leotard and swimsuit, respectively, they postponed hugs. Emily wasn't there. She was wrapping up business with her landlord, getting clear of her apartment. She would be staying at the house with them from now until they left. The young ladies hustled back into the studio after that brief word.

Fran and Denise walked in the front door, to their surprise. Grinning, they hugged them, but before they could say much, Stef popped in, looking smug.

"Sorry, guys, but they're here to see me, not you," she announced with a smile. "They decided to come see what we do, and evaluate whether they might be bold enough to learn what we can teach them for self-defense." She looked at them. "I'm not sure what caused them to reconsider, but I'm glad they did."

"Well," Fran admitted slowly, "Actually, Andrew convinced me to look into it. He worries about us. In his line of work, he sees a lot of ugly things. He doesn't want us to become victims. He says he can defend himself, but what works for him won't work for someone without his size and power. The things you can teach are more likely to help us, he thinks."

Stef laughed and looked at Erin. "I think you made an impression!"

Erin grinned, "True, but you rely on your strength too, maybe as much as Andrew."

"I know, that's why they'll be watching Pam and Dani at work. Who better to demonstrate viable techniques for average-size women than those two?"

Nodding in agreement, Erin assured their waitress friends, "You're in good hands, ladies. What they do *will* work for you. Stefanie is practical, patient, one of the best teachers I've ever seen. She will equip you well. Remember, you're among friends!"

Stef led them back to the studio. As the door closed, Allen held his Genie's hand with a little smile. "If only they had an entourage to defend them!"

She cracked up. "Yeah, well, not everyone gets to be a VIP, my love. Keep in mind we don't just watch over you. We have each other's backs, too."

"I'm glad. I'd have a tough time with any of you getting

hurt, you know?" he admitted.

"I know," she kissed him. "We love you, too."

A few minutes later, some of the other wrestlers started trickling out, freshly showered, to start their weekend. Among them was Laurie, happy to hug them now that she was cleaned up. She talked about the text from Alissa, her visits with her mother, and the waitresses' initial reaction to seeing Pam and Dani in action! Though she only saw their initial reaction before hitting the showers, the gymnast was still cracking up at the shock on their faces. She said they couldn't look away!

As a grown woman, she was getting to know her mother in a way she never had before. It did help to understand the older woman's new conciliatory attitude toward her daughter. Regrets had nearly eaten her alive until Laurie re-entered her life. Edna validated it was true. Her mother listened when Laurie talked about the way Jesus had changed her perspective. While she didn't share her belief, she appreciated how it moved her daughter to forgive her.

They suggested gifting her a Bible. Laurie lit up at the idea! She planned to pick one up before her next visit. She did a lot of listening when she went there, but they encouraged her to share some of the testimonies she had heard when her mother ran out of things to say. Christ is hope, they reminded her. Certainly, Evelyn could use some! Their girl readily agreed.

A bit later, Fran and Denise came out of the studio, shaking their heads. Erin asked what they thought and Laurie grinned. Fran stuck her hand out to Allen. He took it hesitantly, unsure what she meant by the gesture.

She shook it with a smile. "Allen, you're a *brave man* to commit to a woman who can do things like we just saw in there!" Erin laughed.

He looked at his wife fondly. "She's *good* to me, Fran. No matter what she *could* do, she's kind, patient, and loving for my sake. She reminds me of Jesus. I mean that!"

Erin beamed at him, "My Sweet Talker!" Giving him a squeeze at the waist, she looked at the others. "Before we married, I told him he presented a different kind of challenge than any other man I'd met. Instead of breaking him down, it was in my heart to *build him up*. I saw greatness in him! Wanting everyone else to see what I saw, I made up my mind to be the strong woman he needed to stand by him to make it happen!"

Fran replied, "Did you know there's a word in the Bible for that?" He nodded, but Erin shook her head no. "Edify: that's the word Paul used in his letters. He told us to edify one another, building each other up in our most holy faith."

Erin was surprised, "But I made that decision before Jesus saved me! How could I have known, then?"

"It was that supernatural love He placed in your heart for me, Genie," he said softly. "You wanted only good for me, couldn't bear the thought of hurting me, remember?"

"I do. I love teasing you, but hurting you would hurt *me*. I don't even like thinking about it. I love you too much!"

"Me, too, Mom," Laurie wrapped her up in a sympathetic hug, which Erin returned with a smile.

"I'm not sure if I'm brave or not, Fran. Like with Jesus, I'm drawn to her so powerfully I can't help myself. I trust them both, though either could crush me. I'm a fool, yet I am still convinced I couldn't be in better hands. Life without either of them wouldn't be worth living!"

"Well, neither are going to forsake you, nor will we," Denise spoke up. Fran nodded in emphatic agreement. "We're taking up Stef's offer to teach us to protect ourselves. It might not be ladylike, but it's better than getting victimized! Besides, we want to be able to protect people who can't defend themselves!"

Stef entered the living room in time to hear what Denise said. She was elated, "That's the kind of thing I like to hear! Do any of you have dinner plans?"

They didn't. When Dani and Pam came in, she asked

them, too. Dani did not, but Pam said Win made plans for them. Stef wanted to take them all out for dinner. She said teaching self-defense would be a fulfilling change of pace from the normal day-to-day routine, so she felt like celebrating!

CHAPTER 25

Six went out with her: Erin, Allen, Fran, Denise, Laurie, and Dani. Stef sent a text inviting Andrew in appreciation for encouraging the waitresses to take up her offer, but he was working. He stated he'd see everyone at the cookout the next day, though. Emily was contacted, too. She said she'd have to pass, but would see them later at the house. Stef took them to a small ethnic Romanian restaurant, saying it was the closest thing she found locally to the kind of cuisine she grew up eating.

It was educational! The owners knew her well, so she frequented the place, but of those present, only Erin had ever been there with her before. Stef kept her personal life private, which caused Allen to appreciate her sharing this experience with them. The food was okay, but not really his thing; still, it made for a memorable one-time event. The ladies agreed it reminded them of Greek food. He filed away a thought that he was definitely not Greek, then!

There were plenty of veggies to satisfy the female palate. It became apparent Stef noticed he was picking at his food when she commented on it. He was embarrassed, not meaning to be rude, and apologized.

She laughed, saying something to the wait staff he didn't make out. A moment later, two platters of something resembling baked chicken were brought out by the grinning chef, the owner's wife. It was roasted partridge, common fare where they were from. Stef had them hold it back as a prank, knowing how he loved meat!

"Allen, did you think I'd let you starve?" she chided him with a grin. He shrugged, returning her smile. "Don't you know bodybuilders thrive on protein? I need meat even more than you do! Eat your fill, more is coming."

He did. It was *wonderful*! This was something he'd be happy to have again. All were amused at how Stef got him, especially Denise and Laurie. Their hostess wasn't kidding, either. She consumed a platter plus of the game by herself! The owners said it was all you can eat, but Stefanie never failed to impress them with how much she could put away. Grinning, she flexed a huge bicep, pointing out you can't build muscle like *this* without food like that!

Noting how their waitress friends' eyes popped out, Dani added, "Yeah, and an *exhausting* amount of work with the weights, too. Don't scare off your students, boss!"

Stef quickly stated there was no way their bodies would come to resemble hers by accident. A build like Dani's or Erin's would result from working out, at most. A sigh of relief went up since both were strong, yet unmistakably feminine. Fran and Denise did not wish to lose that!

Allen was curious, "Stef, I don't mean to cause trouble, but may I ask who's stronger, you or Laurie?" With a dimpled grin, Laurie just shook her head.

"Naww, that won't cause trouble, Allen. It's pretty close, actually. I think I'm slightly stronger, overall, because I'm so much bigger. I have 8.5 inches and nearly seventy pounds on her, so I can lift more. Pound for pound, though, she's definitely stronger! I can't bend horseshoes like she does. Her bone structure and training have endowed her with freakishly strong hands, which is not a bad thing. I'm a better wrestler, due to experience. My strength doesn't give me an advantage over her." They exchanged a smile. "Believe me, that's not usually the case!"

"I believe you. Erin's made a believer out of me!" The whole table laughed. Erin patted his knee under the table, grinning. They had a good time together, learning a lot about the lands and people north of Turkey. Erin had some experience as a world traveler, but he had never been outside the U.S., other than to walk across the border into Mexico. Hearing Stef reminisce with the restaurant owners gave them some idea of what life was like in those faraway places.

All agreed, though, that they had no desire to return, other than for visits. America was their home now, by their own choice. Their appreciation of the freedoms Americans tend to take for granted caused those present to review how blessed they were to reside here. Not everyone experiences the liberty people have in this nation!

Erin lined up plans with Dani and Laurie to go shopping in the morning for the cookout. She correctly assumed Allen would prefer not to go. Emily would be resting from her long day today, so he would not be alone. Stef had plans that would take her away Saturday overnight. She would return Sunday.

Everyone Christ had united with them in faith planned to attend, to Allen's amazement! As he thought about it, something dropped into his heart he knew came from the Lord: *"They are coming to meet with Me, child."* That being the case, something momentous would be forthcoming in their gathering, he concluded.

It coalesced in his thoughts just as his gaze connected with Fran's. Wondering if the Lord would again confirm His words by her, he grinned. She cocked her head quizzically, the corners of her mouth turning up with the hint of a smile. With a slight nod, he looked away, suddenly sure that indeed He would.

Alone at the house later, he was accosted by his very observant Genie. When he sat on the loveseat, she straddled him. Putting her arms around his neck, her eyes drilled into his, "Okay, buddy, spill it! God showed you something at dinner, didn't He?"

"Wow," he laughed, "*Nothing* gets by you. If I sought to surprise you, like with a party or something, can you advise me how to do it successfully?"

Grinning, she shook her head, "I don't think you can, dear. I read you like a book! I just don't think you can hide anything from me."

"Me, neither," he admitted with a chuckle. A passionate kiss scattered his thoughts, but the challenging sparkle in her eyes when she finished gave him notice that the inquisition had begun! "Whoa! You don't have to do that! I'll tell you everything, I promise!"

She laughed heartily, "*Of course* you will, Sweet Talker. I have ways of making you talk! Even when you do, that doesn't guarantee I'll stop!"

"There's not much to tell. I was thinking how unbelievable it seemed that the whole family Jesus has added to us here is coming tomorrow. It seemed He dropped a thought into my mind that they are coming to meet with Him."

"That makes sense, I guess. Why the funny grin at Fran?"

"Our eyes met across the table. Suddenly, I wondered if He would confirm His word by her, again. It struck me as funny, so I smiled. I think it confused her."

She nodded, "Yup, I think so, too. I'm pretty sure no harm was done, but you need to be careful in the future of things like that. Some women might think you were flirting."

"You don't think Fran..." he was horrified at the thought.

She shook her head, "No, I don't think she took it that way. She didn't look disturbed by your smile, just curious. God may show her what He revealed to you *because* her curiosity leads her to ask Him what that was about. *She's a waitress,* love. She's used to being hit on, and knows when a guy doesn't mean anything by his actions.

"Truthfully, I don't think any of our group would take you the wrong way. A misunderstanding with a stranger isn't hard to imagine, though. If someone doesn't know what motivates a kind gesture, she may jump to the wrong conclusion. You would be mortified if she responded to what she perceived as your advances. Worse, if offended, she might refuse Christ, refuse to hear your witness. A blunder like that would be tough for you to get over."

"That's the truth," he looked her in the eyes. "Erin, I prayed years ago God would take my life before letting me cause someone to miss out on salvation. I do dumb things sometimes, but the idea *I caused someone to turn away from Christ* ... that's more than I can handle. Even giving them reason to stumble ... well, the risk makes me never want to open my mouth again!"

She sat up on his lap, looking down at him. "Had you taken that approach to life, love, how would we have met? How would you have won me to Christ, or any of these others who have come to love you?" He grimaced; she had a point. "Look at it this way: you work for Jesus, right? He is in the business of rescuing the perishing from the sins we are powerless against on our own. Yet, even He can't save everyone, just those who believe what He said enough to trust Him.

"Do you honestly expect to have a better track record than He does?" A rueful smile spread across his face. "His gospel is perfect, husband, but many are offended by it. We're *not* perfect, so it's unrealistic to think we won't offend anyone. Consider Andrew. He is in the lifesaving business, too. He can't save everyone he tries to help, but how many would he save if *he stopped trying?*"

Shaking his head, he stated the obvious, "None."

"Then you shouldn't stop, either." Her smile was encouraging. "You're doing the best you can, following the Spirit of God. It's having an effect, or I wouldn't be pinning you to this sofa right now, would I?" That got him laughing. She grinned, highlighting her point by leaning forward to kiss him. "Don't worry about what might go wrong, love. Trust the Lord. He will keep making us fruitful while working out any mistakes you make for good. Am I right?"

Before he could answer, she covered his lips with hers in another kiss that made it hard to think. The mischievous sparkle in her eyes reminded him her interrogation wasn't finished. He couldn't help laughing, which cracked her up.

"Yes, ma'am, you are absolutely right," he got out as quickly as he could. Another kiss melted the remainder of his resistance as Emily walked in the front door to catch them in the act.

CHAPTER 26

A shocked smile covered her face as both of theirs went red. "Uh, should I come back later?" she chuckled.

Erin rose abruptly, "No, you're fine, honey. I was just... going over some things with Dad." A little smile betrayed her, which put one on his face.

Emily giggled as she looked at them, "I can see that." She set down two suitcases, then moved to hug Erin. When Allen didn't stand, Emily looked at him curiously.

He went bright red, embarrassed. Spreading his arms wide, he invited an embrace from his seated position. "It's good to see you, but I'm just so comfortable that I'm not prepared to get up yet. Sorry!"

Erin burst out laughing. Emily looked at her a moment, then back at him. Her jaw dropped open and a loud giggle came out.

Her gaze turned away from him when Erin declared, "You caught us, sweetie. It won't be the last time, either, since you're coming to live with us. We're not exhibitionists, but we *are* very affectionate and I'm not shy about how I feel toward him. I hope that's not too awkward for you!"

Grinning from ear to ear, their girl walked around behind the sofa, then leaned over to put her cheek against his. Her arms wrapped around his neck in a hug as she chuckled, "If you're *that* comfortable, Dad, don't get up on my account. I'm glad you're enjoying your visit here!"

She giggled again as he replied, "I am. Thank you for understanding. Did you get things wrapped up, so you're ready to go home with us?" It made for a good diversion. Erin sat beside him, patting his knee with a smile, while Emily settled on the couch.

"Yes, I did. I didn't realize how much stuff I had until I began to clear it all out! It has a way of piling up without being noticed, as you find places to put it away. It's a good thing I didn't get too attached to it!"

"Good for you! I can tell you from experience, that will simplify moving every time. Have you sold your car yet?"

"Yes, my friend just dropped me here and took it. I'm afoot, with you guys from now on until we get home. Home! I can't tell you what that means to me! To have a place surrounded by family, a place where I feel safe and welcome, no longer alone… it's a dream come true! Thank you so much for making room for me!"

He shook his head, "There's no need to thank us, Emily. We love you! We're thrilled the Lord worked it out this way."

"I know how you feel," Erin commented. "Growing up without parents, believe me, *I know*. That I can help alleviate some of that for you and a few others is very satisfying to me. Having this man I love at my side to share it with me, though… it's perfect! There's just no other word to describe the grace God is showing me. I thank Him all the time for it!" She winked at Emily, then gave him a mischievous smile, "Also, I make my man as *comfortable* as I can, so he doesn't even want to get up!"

When they finished laughing, Emily ruminated, "Actually, I've been paying close attention to how you two interact. I'm looking forward to observing you in your own home. You are modeling what a loving couple's relationship should be. I haven't been exposed to that. Not being a child anymore, it's too late for you to tell me what to do, but you are showing me by example life lessons I never received while growing up."

"Now *that's* proactive," he sat up straight and glanced at Erin. "Remember how Pam asked us to write a book advising about relationships?" She nodded. "I wonder what she would think about Emily's approach. Instead of waiting for a book, she just moves in to observe us firsthand!"

Emily began to laugh so hard that it turned into tears. It got Erin, too. Once she recovered, she commented, "I think we ought to ask her. She'll get a kick out of it. No question, it's a bold approach!"

They visited a while longer before retiring for the night. It was late and Erin had shopping plans in the morning. Emily rescued him from interrogation, but he learned Erin had a bigger endgame in mind after they were alone in their room. There was no way out of it, even if he wanted to find one, which he didn't. They slept like rocks, afterward!

She was gone when he woke the next morning. After getting ready for the day, he opened the door to the smell of breakfast Emily was cooking for them. Erin, Dani, and Laurie left half an hour ago, she said. It was nearly 10 a.m. Emily had been up about an hour and decided to make breakfast. He thanked her and they ate together.

The one on one time was nice. It occurred to him that of the four young ladies he had come to view as his girls, he knew this one the least, so he enjoyed the opportunity to get better acquainted with her. It seemed she did, too. She wouldn't let him help clean up, but was glad he stuck around to keep her company. Stef left earlier that morning, saying only she'd be back tomorrow. Em and Allen were alone.

He inquired as to what kind of work she would look for in Missouri. She wasn't particular, she said. She was thinking about taking some college courses, perhaps in engineering or graphic design. Putting things together to make something intricate fascinated her. She had an appreciation for structures that reflected detailed thought. That's why the mini golf course intrigued her. Puzzles drew her in. She liked to solve them, but creating them appealed to her, too.

He and his mom shared a love of stories, particularly mysteries, he informed her. Did she like to read? A little embarrassed, she said she wasn't very good at it. She liked stories, but television and movies were easier to follow. He remembered whatever education she received was on the far side of the world, where she grew up. Suggesting she take a remedial reading course before starting other classes, he also offered to read stories with her, for enjoyment and to improve her skills. She loved the idea!

When she seemed ashamed about needing help, he nipped that in the bud. "Emily, how many languages do you speak?"

"Well... four, actually," she said, "Traditional, Ukrainian, Russian, and English."

His eyes widened, "Whoa! What is traditional?"

"It was what the People spoke when I was a child. Some called it *Romani*, others *Vlax*. It was natural to me then; I'm rusty in it now. I haven't used it in a long time."

He grinned at her, "Girl, that's three more languages than I speak!" She smiled. "You have nothing to be ashamed of. English is not your native tongue, anyway. You speak it fluently, you just need to finish learning how to read and write it. We can help with that. Would you like to get your GED?"

"You think I could?"

"Absolutely! We'll help you. You'll need it before

taking college classes." Her face lit up. "I think it's very cool that we have a translator in the family, you know?"

She laughed in delight, and gave him a sideways hug, "Thanks, Dad! I've never had anyone tell me I can do what I set out to do! I'm so excited!"

He chuckled, "You better get used to it, sweetie, because that's what family does. We encourage and support one another. Heidi and Ruth will help you, too. How are you at math?"

"I think I'm pretty good. I've been handling my own finances ever since I left the People. I budgeted all by myself to hire a lawyer, remember?" He nodded. She lowered her voice, "You know I told you I've been putting money aside for a while, right? Well, consolidated with what I made from selling things yesterday, especially the car, I'm taking a little more than thirteen thousand dollars to start my new life in Missouri." She was obviously pleased.

"Good for you! I'm proud of you, and also flattered you trust me enough to tell me. Are you carrying all that on you in cash?"

"No, that wouldn't be smart. Mostly, it's in traveler's checks, fully insured against loss or theft. It's as safe as I know how to make it!"

"Sounds like you did good. Stay close to Mom and me while we're traveling, okay?"

"I was already planning to, for safety's sake. Any other advice?"

"I think you've got things well in hand already. Erin is used to having money, so you might ask her, but otherwise keep it to yourself how much you're carrying." She grinned. "I didn't have to tell *you* that, did I?" She shook her head.

Not long afterward, the garage door opened, letting them know shopping was finished. Juanita and Carlos arrived while they brought in groceries. They were eager to see them. Additionally, Carlos planned to help Dani with the grilling.

Allen had a thought. Taking Laurie aside, he asked if she had considered inviting her mother to join them, if she felt up to it. She said Evelyn preferred black tie events, sneering at less formal gatherings, but decided to send her a text message anyway.

Minutes later, the response came. When should she arrive? Laurie was shocked. Erin laid a hand on her shoulder, saying the invitation was probably accepted because she was the one extending it. The little titan chewed that over and grew unusually quiet as she sent the reply. She didn't seem to understand how her parent valued the second chance Laurie afforded her.

1:00 p.m. was the time set to meet. It didn't matter. Their hearts were knit together so their brethren started arriving a bit before noon. Andrew, Fran, and Denise came in together, singles having found comfort in friendship and shared company. Reina joined them, then Guillermo, Carol and her husband, Tom. Pam and Win came in about 12:40, followed closely by Teresa.

Edna was with Evelyn when they parked ten minutes later. A bit pale, she wore a sweater despite the warmth, but her eyes and her smile were bright. They gave her a warm welcome. She soaked up their hospitality. Alissa texted Erin they had arrived, both her family and Ted's. Emily met them at the door and brought them to the backyard.

Introductions were made all around. Alissa immediately passed out hugs, starting with Teresa, Erin, and Allen, then the three musketeers. Hans identified his boss, Ted, his wife, Liz, and their sons, Eli and Conrad. Eli was nineteen, a freshman in college, while Conrad was sixteen. All the kids struck Allen as very intelligent.

They got acquainted as they ate. There was no sign of the outraged Hans who left the gym in a huff last Sunday. Allen was curious as to what changed, but it seemed best to let him broach matters in his own way. As all were getting full, Hans discarded his plate and began his tale.

CHAPTER 27

He was thorough, starting with how Allen's words angered him, then the discussion with his daughter after he cooled off. When his edict didn't draw ire from Alissa, he admitted it surprised him. Then he described his inexplicable escape from the pile-up on the foggy freeway the next morning. Incredulous stares met his description of the event on all sides!

Andrew interrupted, "You were *in* that? I worked that accident, Hans. I've had nightmares about it ever since! The first semi-driver was in critical condition when we retrieved him, but the second was badly mangled. He never had a chance. Sandwiched between them in a two-seat sports car… you shouldn't be here now!"

"I can't explain it," Hans shook his head slowly. "I closed my eyes, bracing for impact, then opened them to find myself on the other side of the pile-up. All I can think is, the glowing figure in the passenger seat somehow took us *through* it. The big groove inches from where I was sitting prevented me from deciding I imagined the whole thing."

He continued, describing how he and Alma struggled to come to grips with what happened. He told them of the scripture on Ted's calendar that read like an ultimatum to him, then the question he posed alone in his car the next day aloud, with its unexpected answer: *"My daughter is praying for you."* The thought was comforting until he examined it further to realize *it wasn't his*!

He remembered Allen distinguished how she had a *heavenly* Father, as well as an earthly father. This unseen God was not only staking a claim on Alissa, He was *proud* of her! Her eyes glistened as the group smiled at her.

He became curious enough to consider swallowing his pride, and maybe give Allen a call. It was the first reaction Evelyn had; she smiled. She understood pride all too well! Other than Andrew's early interjection, no one interrupted Hans. Even the teens were spellbound! It was Wednesday before he tried to call, unaware the couple was out of touch in the wilderness.

He went on to describe falling on his face as he sought to catch an elevator, only to discover a few minutes later that particular elevator car plummeted to its destruction. It made the news, being such an odd event in a government building, but Hans' close call was known only to him and those he shared it with, which included only present company.

By this time, he was convinced the glowing figure glimpsed in his peripheral vision at each incident was *protecting* him, sparing his life. If God wasn't sending him aid, then who was? He wasn't escaping death unscathed, but at least he *survived*. The events weren't typical of daily life, but they weren't supernatural, either. These things happen. His continued survival was what defied explanation.

Unsure where to seek counsel, he decided to tell his family everything, even his conclusions. Alissa remembered what Allen said, that God would prove Himself three times this week, stipulating it couldn't happen unless he was alive to see it. He couldn't find fault with her logic, having been miraculously preserved twice already. He felt like a dead man walking! Her words were the only comfort he could find.

Thursday morning at work, he read the scripture on Ted's calendar. His boss was kind enough to elaborate on what it meant. One thing led to another, until he confided all that had happened to him. Ted was appalled! He advised meeting with Allen, and also asking if he could join them. That's how they ended up with them today.

Ted spoke up, while those listening were still trying to absorb all Hans told them. "Allen, I don't know what your beliefs are, but you seem to know something of what God is doing. I can't stay away from that kind of insight! I've wanted Him to make use of me, but the best direction I received was to buy Hans a Bible a few weeks ago. I did, then chickened out about giving it to him, afraid it might offend him. I finally gave it to him Thursday, when he asked what the scripture on my desk meant."

"I'm not very bold, but I want to serve my Redeemer in a meaningful way. I guess I came along to see if He can use me. Of course, I'm also concerned about what's been happening with Hans."

"Ted, I love your heart! The answer is yes and amen! We'll get back to this, but I have the impression Hans has a little more to tell us. Were you finished, Hans?"

A sly smile belied his features, "How did you know there was more?"

He shook his head, "I didn't. You have only described two proofs the Lord has given you of Himself, so far. He indicated there would be three. The third could still be coming, but you don't seem desperate for an explanation right now, so I'm thinking it has been provided to you."

"You are correct. I misjudged you at first, thinking you

were some kind of hillbilly yokel. I was wrong! My daughter's judgment was better than mine. As I reclined after dinner last night, it was as if I stood in her room near the foot of her bed. She knelt there praying, her brother at her side. Someone stood beside me. I couldn't see Him, however, I heard Him speak, *"My children are praying for you."*

"I knew immediately Erik had received Christ, too." Both kids were wide-eyed. Erik's jaw looked like it might hit the floor! Hans just smiled at them with adoration. "As I watched, Alma came to the door, hesitated a moment, then joined them. The Presence at my side told me, *"My family is gathering to Me. The time for nonsense is past. You may join them in coming to Me, but I will not permit you to come between us. Make your choice!"*

"If I did not believe Him, we wouldn't be here today. I'm certain *I* wouldn't survive another week without Christ! There is no fear in me, though, because I *do* believe in Him. I still live, by His preference. He has been kind, showing me my grace period to make a decision for Him is ending. Since He proved Himself to me, I am ready to prove His mercy toward me has not been in vain!"

He took Alma's hand, "I think *we* are ready." She nodded. "Would you lead us to Christ, Allen?"

"I'd be honored." he glanced over at Evelyn. She was watching but made no move, so he instructed the couple to repeat this prayer:

"Lord Jesus, I am a sinner. My sins have kept me from You, even though they were committed in ignorance. You paid the death penalty they warranted, when You died on the cross at Calvary. When You rose from the dead, You made eternal life available for all who trust in You.

I place my trust in You from this day forward, living for You from now on. Please forgive me and establish me to walk in righteousness from now on, that I might please You, rather than myself. In Jesus' name, I pray. Amen."

Laurie let out a delighted whoop that got everyone laughing! Alissa and Erik embraced their parents, absolutely thrilled. Ted and Eli high-fived, grinning. Tears streaked several faces and smiles abounded. One of those tear-streaked faces was Andrew's.

"It's about time something good came out of that mess on Monday," he reflected. "I guess I needed to see that." Fran's arm went around him sympathetically.

Hans looked at him, then at Erin and Allen, "The way I see it, I died that day on the freeway. My Miata was my coffin; if I want to live in Christ, I can't keep it. It symbolizes my old life. If I repaired it, I'd be tempted to hang on to it. Does that make any sense?" Alma hugged him, clearly pleased. He chuckled, "She never liked that car, called it a deathtrap."

"It does," Allen told him. "For you, putting it behind you serves the same purpose as water baptism. The old life is forfeited, so the new life in Christ can be embraced."

Carol's husband Tom spoke up, "Allen, is that Biblical?" Denise watched him closely. He remembered she had Baptist roots.

"Let me ask you this, Tom: is water baptism for our benefit, or God's?"

He thought a moment, "I'm not really sure. We do it because we're following the example Jesus set for us."

"Before Jesus started His ministry, John came preaching a baptism of repentance. People were called to repent and baptism was the sign embraced to show they did. People, particularly Jews, seek a sign, so God provides signs. Signs are for our benefit. God has no need for them, since He knows our hearts."

"That sign shook ancient Israel. Under the Law of Moses, animal sacrifices were the only way to atone for sin before God. John taught God was sending His own Son as the final sacrifice for all sin. Whoever put his faith in Him would be justified, once and for all! Jews under the Law understood that, though some rejected it."

"Baptism signified their acceptance of God's grace. Going under the water was as though they died with Christ, then were raised with Him by faith, through no effort of their own. It prepared them to receive Him."

"I'm afraid it often isn't seen that way, nowadays. It has become a religious ritual, a rite of passage for membership in some denominations. If it means something to the one being baptized, great, but if it is only done because they think people expect it of them, it serves no purpose.

"Immersing Hans could not provide a more jarring taste of death than he experienced this past Monday! In his own words, he has felt like a "dead man walking" until he received new life in Christ, just now. He could elect to be baptized, if God puts it in his heart; otherwise, it's just not necessary."

Denise put in, "Then why did Jesus set the example, Allen? You *do* know how vital baptism is to Baptists, don't you?"

"Yes, I do," he chuckled. "It symbolizes repentance, without which there is no forgiveness of sins. Because repentance is vital, Jesus endorsed the symbol. As the One without sin, did He need to repent?"

"*No,*" she shook her head emphatically. A handful of others did, too.

"Jesus preached repentance, with the need to trust in Him, throughout His ministry. However, He only baptized at the Jordan for a short time, just long enough to exceed the number of those baptized by John. He endorsed what John was doing, but His ministry was greater. He baptized only long enough to make that point.

"Immersion wasn't vital; repentance *is*. John stated Jesus would provide a *better* baptism than he could offer. You've had both kinds, Denise. Was John right, in your opinion?"

A grin spread across her features, "Yeah, he was, no

question!" There were nods of agreement all around.

CHAPTER 28

Edna spoke up, "Evelyn is tired. This has been quite an outing for her! Thank you all for having us. We've enjoyed it, but it's time for us to go."

Evelyn nodded and gave Laurie's hand an affectionate squeeze. Laurie smiled back. They thanked her for coming, offering to pray for her, but she declined. Her voice was faint. As they reached the gate, Edna stopped, bent down, then stood to face the group.

"Evelyn says even though she can't stay, she would appreciate whatever prayers you are willing to make after we're gone, and says thank you." They assured them they would indeed pray for her. Laurie walked them out.

Conrad asked what was wrong with her, looking at Alissa. Her mother answered the question when she hesitated to speak. Everyone was silent for a moment.

Ted looked at Allen, "Does she know Christ?"

"Not yet, but He's working on her," he replied. "Besides, Laurie's witness is not easy to ignore." Their girl stepped out on the porch in time to catch what he said. She flashed a half-smile at him. He smiled back, as Erin took his hand.

Hans settled back into his chair. "So now that we live for Christ, what's next, Allen? I really don't know what to do."

"*Commit your way unto the Lord and He will direct your path*," scripture says. Your chief interaction with Him is prayer. Tell Him what is in your heart: the more you do, the more you will be filled with His peace. He will speak to you through scripture and directly into your spirit. As you devote time to Him, His desires will become your own. We use daily conference calls to stay in touch and study the Bible together."

His eyebrows went up, "You don't attend a church?" Alma, Ted, and Liz mirrored his expression of surprise.

"Guys, we *are* a church, just not in a traditional sense. We're broken people Christ has rescued, bound together at the heart and made into family. Every church I've ever been in has a "this close, but no closer" mentality that keeps most everyone at arm's length, with the exception of some cliques. Our testimonies have drawn us together much closer than that! We don't want to be separated, because among these people, we *know* we are loved. Am I right?" Hearty agreement came from every direction.

Tom was thoughtful, "I know what you mean about the distance between parishioners. Putting their best foot forward in church, it's like they're afraid if you get to know them well, you might find out they are less than perfect in real life, so they withdraw. Church can be a lonely place. It shouldn't be that way, but it is."

"I agree. Facades are like walls people hide behind for protection. It's a very human defense mechanism with one big failing; how can you reach someone else without exposing yourself? It's not possible.

"We are told in Ephesians to put on the whole armor of God, instead. It will protect us while allowing us to reach out to others in need with the love of Christ our Lord. Meeting needs and pleasing Him; isn't that what we're called to do?"

Hans nodded slowly, "I wondered how I could trust ministers I've viewed with disdain all my adult life. Even after concluding Jesus is real, having bowed my knee to Him, money seems to be their primary motivation. That doesn't inspire my trust, just suspicion, but you're not asking for money. I think I can trust you, Allen."

"Darn! I was about to ask if you could spare a quarter," he quipped. It cracked everyone up! "Actually, I consider that high praise, Hans. Thank you!"

"Okay," Carol piped up mischievously, "I've been waiting to see the reaction when this comes up, but since it hasn't, *I'll* bring it up. If this place *isn't* a church, what is it?"

Laughing, Allen shook his head, "You're a rabble-rouser, Carol!" Smiles and laughter were everywhere amongst their group, while the two new families and Tom looked on curiously. The lone exception was Alissa, who grinned.

Erin announced matter-of-factly, "This is the company I founded some years ago, named "A Crushing Experience", A*C*E for short. Women wrestle and defeat guys here who *pay* for the experience. Not to brag, but we're very good at it! We also record and sell videos of select matches."

Shock and disbelief reflected on the newcomer's faces, while Alissa giggled. "Nuh-uh!" came out of Eli's mouth before he thought. It garnered appraising looks from Erin and her employees.

"Young man," Andrew rumbled, his deep voice drawing everyone's attention, "I recommend you don't disrespect these ladies by challenging their claims. I did, the first time I met them, and came to regret it. If you're as foolish as I was, you will, too!"

Liz's disbelief seemed to have some pleasure mixed in,

"May I ask which of you wrestle?"

Pam and the three musketeers raised their hands. Erin narrated, "These are on the active roster. Juanita is on maternity leave. Technically, she could raise her hand, too. I am retired. More than half a dozen are not here right now, including my business partner, who runs the place. Pam assists her. We'll show you the studio if you are interested."

"I don't... get how a business of such... secular interests has become a site where Christ is working so powerfully," Ted tried to wrap his head around it. "It's unprecedented, doesn't even seem possible!"

"It's unique, for sure," Allen exchanged a smile with Erin. "It proves what the Bible says, that nothing is too difficult for the Lord." They launched into the story of how He brought the two of them together, winning Erin over to receive salvation in the process. Her encounter with Christ was received in utter silence until she finished.

The kids were fully absorbed. Alma drew a deep breath, "Now *that's* a match made in heaven! It's better than any fairy tale I've heard." Several others agreed. They went on to describe events that followed, up to the attack on Allen and how he was miraculously preserved. Instead of resulting in his demise, Heidi and Laurie received Christ after Heidi's demon was cast out before the entire company!

That caused a stir. Hans shook his head, "My life-changing week has just been another chapter added to the lives you people lead! No wonder you had no trouble believing what I told you."

Conrad addressed Erin, "The hold that big woman, Heidi, used on Allen; was that a rear naked choke?" She affirmed that it was. He shook his head, then looked at his folks, particularly his older brother. "Only God could have kept Allen alive through five or six minutes of that! Eli, if these ladies are proficient in Brazilian Jiu-Jitsu, you *don't* want to question their abilities. They are trained to knock their opponents out!"

"We are," Pam confirmed briefly.

"That's what Erin did to me before I knew what was happening," Andrew intoned soberly. "They have my complete respect now. But those present also happen to be some of the best friends anyone could ever wish for, too!" Allen's entourage lit up with bright smiles in response, along with Pam.

Alissa spoke up to tell everyone about Heidi, how she was caring for Allen's elderly mother in their absence, and the amazing friendship the two of them had. The change in the tall Amazon who nearly killed him bowled both families over! Erin and Allen mentioned they would become acquainted with her if they joined in the conference call gatherings, going forward.

Tom had not spoken in a while, but he stepped forward. "Allen, for two decades I've attended our Methodist church. I've never seen anything like what we heard about here today! Carol told me how she received the Holy Spirit baptism among you. I couldn't reconcile it with what we were taught, but the deliverance Guillermo received and the change in my wife was undeniable. Since it is not in man to do these things, it *has* to be God at work! Might I obtain this baptism, as well?"

Laurie giggled with joy, which brought several chuckles from the rest of them. Allen cast a grin her way. She moved next to him, wrapping him up in a hug.

"How about it? Is anyone else ready to receive the Spirit of God that empowers us?"

Hans and Alma were at a loss. They had no idea what he was talking about. Before they could say anything, though, Liz and Ted exchanged a quick look, then she spoke.

"We're Nazarene, Allen. We already have the Holy Spirit. If you're talking about speaking in tongues, we don't believe in that."

"Do you believe it ever happened?"

"Huh?"

"In the book of Acts, where the Day of Pentecost was described, do you believe the account in scripture, that they spoke in tongues then?"

"Well, of course, we believe the Bible!" she flustered.

"That's good to hear. What did the bystanders declare they heard them speaking in their own languages?"

Ted spoke, "They said the Jews were praising and glorifying God, Allen. It was a marvelous sign, at the time. Onlookers wondered if they were drunk, but it didn't make sense, even when they posed the idea. Getting drunk never makes people *more* coherent! It certainly doesn't magically grant fluency in foreign languages, either."

"So the utterance had to come from the indwelling Holy Spirit, rather than those believers, right?" They nodded. "It is written, *"I am the Lord; I change not."* Jesus Christ is the same yesterday, today, and forever. Why would the indwelling Spirit of Truth praise and glorify God with the lips of people then, yet cease to do so later? Did He decide to withhold praise, at some point?"

They seemed uncertain. "That doesn't make sense," Ted conceded.

"We bring the sacrifice of praise"; you're familiar with that passage, I'm sure. Some say it means we offer thanksgiving when we don't feel like it, like when we're having a hard time. How can we praise Him when it's just not in us? *We sacrifice our lips to let Him speak from our heart.* That's our sacrifice. He supplies the praise."

"He even intercedes for us with groanings that cannot be uttered when our pain defies our ability to describe it. The "we" that brings the sacrifice of praise isn't a multitude of worshippers. It's the believer in Christ and the Spirit of God empowering them, working together in tandem to supply what pleases God and releases His power!"

Erik said something to his sister, who smiled and

nodded. He then got up to stand beside Tom. Allen looked at him curiously.

He grinned, "I don't know exactly what this is, but Alissa says she's got it. If my sister has it, it must be good, so I want it, too!" There was laughter, but Allen assured him the Lord would honor his request. He does not withhold any good thing from those who ask.

Hans stood, looking sheepish. "My children have displayed more wisdom this past week than I have. I am going to trust them, this time." Alma stood beside him with a smile.

Eli stood, "Mom, Dad, I have to see if there is something to this. If nothing happens, I haven't lost anything, but I need to see for myself, you know?" Ted pursed his lips. Liz's face was almost grim. Conrad seemed torn between them and his brother, but he did not move.

Allen told Ted, "It's up to you. The Holy Spirit is a gentleman. He doesn't force Himself on anyone, nor does this change the salvation you have obtained in Christ. You came here, curious about the power of God you heard was working in us. The infilling, baptism, whatever you want to call it, of the Holy Spirit is the secret behind that power."

"Only you can decide if you're ready to receive it, to lend Him your lips. There is no pressure, my brother in Christ, and no penalty for waiting." He nodded once; it seemed as though he and Liz heaved a sigh of relief.

CHAPTER 29

Allen stood before them, Erin on one side, Laurie on the other, their hands in his. Directing those before them to join hands, he called Carol to stand with Tom, Alissa to stand with her family and Denise to come forward, then addressed Eli.

"Since those closest to you have not received this baptism, I'd like to ask Denise to stand with you, if that's okay. She comes from a Baptist background. Their beliefs are similar to the Nazarene, in this matter. Christ has proven Himself to her, despite it! Is that okay with both of you?"

Both were pleased to stand together. Knowing Hans and Alma did not know what to do, he prayed a very basic prayer for them all. He thanked Jesus for His grace in saving them and His gifts to enable them to stand in faith, while maintaining the purity and holiness with which He had covered them. Stillness settled over the yard.

He instructed those before him, "If you want His Spirit, all you have to do is ask Him to please fill you now, then begin to thank Him." He raised his voice, "Let everyone here with the breath of life praise the Lord, for He is certainly worthy of praise!"

They did. They weren't quiet about it, either -- it was like a dam bursting. The more they worshipped, the more they *wanted* to worship Him! Praise, thanksgiving, and tongues mingled in an outpouring from their hearts that just kept flowing. A hot whirlwind sprang up to engulf them where they stood, spreading outward, then dissipated. Several dropped to their knees, overcome at the visitation of the Lord. Ted and Liz were among them, coming off their chairs to hit their knees!

Hans was on the grass, weeping. Alma knelt with her arm around him. Conrad got up to embrace his brother. Both were crying, thanking God and Denise for standing with them. She was crying and laughing at the same time. A lot of that was going around! Win caught Allen's eye. He had resettled into a chair with an astonished look on his face.

Pam seemed to be at a loss. The Lord dropped something into his heart. Pointing out his destination to Erin, Allen guided Laurie along with him to Juanita, then beckoned her to join them. Carlos followed as they approached Pam. Win was speaking in tongues nonstop, they heard as they drew close, getting the biggest kick out of what was coming out of his mouth!

Allen asked Pam if they could pray for her. She hesitated, seeing the group with him, then nodded. Having her sit down, he asked Laurie and Juanita to each lay a hand on her shoulder, praying in tongues. Erin's hand in his, Carlos holding her other hand, he took Pam's hand, "Lord Jesus, please fill her with your Spirit."

In an instant, she looked as though she'd been turned into the Energizer bunny, almost as if being supercharged as they watched! She *shook* in the chair until her lips trembled, then commenced spewing in tongues like a volcano erupting! Coming up out of the chair, she bounced in place, laughing, praising God in other tongues the whole time. Juanita and Laurie lapsed into giggles, having to sit down themselves. Carlos settled next to Juanita, praising God and smiling.

Andrew's laughter drew their attention. Fran stood by him, grinning. Allen waved both over, asking them to stay close and watch. Emily and Dani drew near when they saw Laurie settle into a chair with the giggles. He dispatched Emily to ask if Gui and Reina would join Carol and Tom to see how they were doing, then sent Dani to guide the boys with Denise near to their parents until they could get to them. Approaching Alissa's family, he noted Teresa was already with her, huge grins on both their faces.

Erik stood by as his parents rose to their feet, their faces flushed, radiant. Hans grinned and stuck his hand out, but Allen shook his head and gripped him in a full embrace! Initially shocked, he returned it after a moment, then stepped back to look at them.

"We're with you from now on, Allen! How could I have gone through life, not knowing this is *real*?"

"The world we live in rejects Christ, Hans. The Bible says the fear of the Lord is the beginning of wisdom. The world values knowledge but lacks wisdom because it has disdained the foundation upon which it is built. Don't berate yourself for missing what was hidden from you by the Deceiver; rejoice that the Lord has opened your eyes to the truth and set you free!"

"A deceiver... then I didn't just overlook the truth about Jesus?"

"No, sir! You fell victim to a massive cover-up, engineered by the Devil himself. The Spirit of Truth abiding in you now will provide discernment, so you won't be fooled again."

He shook his head, "So the Devil is real, too. I guess I have a lot to learn."

Allen grinned, "Don't worry, we're with you from now on, too." That got a smile.

Ted and Liz were back up on their chairs, looking shaken. "Are y'all okay?" he inquired.

Ted shook his head ruefully, "I had to ask. *We* had to ask." Allen cocked his head, unsure what he meant.

"Exactly! That's what happened to me," Win's voice rang out. They turned to look at him. Pam was sitting beside him, looking embarrassed. "That whirlwind came through and before I knew it, I asked God to fill me, too, if this is real. As soon as I did, He did!"

"That's what happened to us, on the money," Liz declared. "That manifestation pushed us over the edge. Suddenly in His presence, we wanted all of God we could get… and got more than we bargained for!"

The ministry team started laughing. It circulated through the gathering like a refreshing breeze.

Pam asked shyly, "Why didn't I get it as easy as Win, Allen? It felt like I was overpowered, in a way, even though I wanted it. I asked at the same time he did."

He chuckled, "Pam, the Lord showed me you are a fighter, through and through! Because of that, there is one thing you're not good at; surrender!" Her coworkers laughed, nodding. "You wanted God to have His way in you, but you didn't know how to submit and let Him. His response was to fill you with so much joy you couldn't contain yourself! With your reserve thrown off-balance, He was able to grant your desire."

"Getting a submission from Pam is worse than pulling teeth," Erin pointed out, laughing. "No offense intended, Win." He chuckled. Pam shrugged, a sheepish grin on her face.

"Well, you know He's tougher than you are, now. You'll learn to trust Him over time," he assured her, "especially with His Spirit abiding in you."

Turning back to Ted and Liz, he added, "Even though

you got more than you bargained for, you made a good decision. God offers the *best* gifts to help us live for Him. If it is His will that we should receive these things, knowing what we will face in this life, can we really afford to reject a part of His provision? You know, in a lot of cultures, rejecting a gift insults the giver."

"You're right there," Liz declared. "I did a stint in the Peace Corps, found out about that personally. Surely God knows we never meant to insult Him!"

"He does. You may have seen His gifts misused, but that doesn't mean He gives them frivolously. Each one is a stewardship. It is a fact that some people are not good stewards. That doesn't mean the *gift* is blemished. Now *you* are entrusted with this stewardship. It is an honor, so strive to be worthy of it, whether others are or not!"

Conrad nodded, "No question, this came from God, even if it puts us on the outs with the Nazarene Church. They were wrong about this… no, *we* were wrong. God has honored us, anyway. Pentecostals act like they are better than us because of this, so we denied the doctrine, but *we* were wrong."

He was surprised, "Conrad, you're a young theologian!"

He smiled, "I know what I believe and why I believe it, Allen. That's all."

"Well, good for you! Don't get hung up about being mistaken. Following Christ is a constant learning process. *"Whom the Lord loves, He chastens,"* remember? Pentecostals who puff up in pride are every bit as wrong, and an attitude adjustment is a more painful correction to receive than a doctrinal deficiency! When everything good that we have comes down from the Father of lights, pride is only justified in the One who has redeemed us so generously."

He turned to Ted once more, "His proximity in that manifestation *moved* you to ask for His gift because you love Him. No one who loves Him does it by measure. We want all of Him we can get! It will be like that for each of us at His appearance. It's the reason you came here, the reason you asked Hans if you could come with him to meet us. You just didn't expect Him to meet you like He did. Tell me, Ted, *who* walks away from His presence unchanged?"

The brightest grin lit his face as he shook his head, "Nobody, Allen. Jesus changes everyone and everything, every time."

"Amen!" came from Tom, Carlos, and Guillermo simultaneously. It shocked them, cracking everyone up.

"I think we have a consensus," Erin observed.

Close at hand, Andrew wondered aloud, "What about the unrepentant? I don't see how Jesus changes them." Folks went silent. Allen recalled how he'd been hurt.

He laid a hand on his shoulder, sympathizing. "That's the opposite side of the coin, my brother. Rejecting Him changes them, too. They become worse and worse. Their hearts are hardened. The last beatitude in Matthew chapter five is for you. Take a look at it when you're alone, okay?" He nodded.

Erin began to explain how the conference call fellowships worked to the newcomers, getting phone numbers and giving them theirs. All expressed they planned to participate, as they were able. It seemed to Allen their number was growing too large to maintain the personal contact with all of them that made the group so unique.

CHAPTER 30

As he thought about it, Fran got his attention. Andrew still stood close, while Danielle had gravitated toward them. The rest were listening to Erin.

"I don't mind that you called me over, Allen, but I didn't do anything. Were you simply trying to include Andrew and me?" Andrew was curious, hearing it. Dani just listened.

"No, ma'am. I wanted you to see what the Lord was doing with me. You watched more closely than you would have out there, didn't you?" Both nodded. "Did you see what motivated the order in which I addressed folks?"

"Not really. Did I miss something?"

"I think you caught more than you know. I prioritized those who needed support the most. All this is completely new to Alissa's family, so I went to Hans first. The rest look to him, so giving him support comforted his wife and kids. Tom had his wife at his side with Gui and Reina backing her up, so I was comfortable leaving them to field his questions. If anything came up they couldn't help him with, I figured they'd approach me later."

"Having addressed Hans, I turned to Ted's family. This really rocked their world! I asked if they were okay, not because I worried for them (we both know the Lord wouldn't hurt them), but to show *I cared*. Their frustration could have walled them off from any attempt to walk them through this, yet the order in which they were addressed showed them everything was okay. It's hard to be offended at someone who honestly cares about you, you know?"

She nodded, but Andrew answered him, "I use the same technique in my job. It works."

"Yes, it does. Their church will probably excommunicate them if they return speaking in tongues. Even Baptists are generally more tolerant of this doctrine than Nazarenes. I don't want them bereft of support, don't want to give Satan that opportunity at them."

Her eyes widened, "You took them in the order of your concern for them."

"You got it! I think I followed the Spirit's leading, but I definitely followed my heart. It was important for you to see that."

"Why?"

"Because you have the heart, the leading of the Holy Spirit, and the understanding of scripture to do what I'm doing, Fran! See how *many* of them there are now? *I need help!* The Word says to teach faithful men, who will also teach faithful men. You fill the bill! You are also *here* when I'm in Missouri. I'd like to teach you to do what I'd do, when I'm not present to do it. I think you will be needed. Are you willing?"

Tears started pouring down her cheeks, "Allen, I-I'm not strong enough!"

"Of course you're not! Neither am I, on my own, but that's just it; *we're not alone*. It is the Lord that does His work. We're just the broken vessels He uses, so that His glory may be plainly seen. He makes the most amazing use of the most broken vessels, remember?"

She shrugged and nodded. Andrew laid a comforting hand the size of a ham on her shoulder.

"Look beside you. Just being your compassionate self, your friendship has helped to shore up Andrew's heart against the devastation that threatened to overwhelm him. You don't understand how much that means! You have befriended a very devoted giant who is determined to have your back, did you know that? Andrew, am I wrong?"

The big man shook his head slowly, a broad grin stretching its way across his face as she looked up at him. "Allen, you're in my head again! Little lady, you have helped me keep my sanity. I don't know much about ministry, but there's *no doubt* in my mind you have what it takes. He's right! Any time the Lord gives you direction, you call me and I'll be there to stand with you, however you need. It's no imposition! I owe you and I *want* you to count on me, understand?" She nodded mutely.

"Can I give you some homework, as my student?" She nodded again with a chuckle. "Look at the story of Deborah and Barak in the book of Judges. This kind of partnership is not without precedent. I'm only a phone call away, too. Trust the Lord, Fran! He won't overload you. You have been a blessing to Denise, then Andrew, just by being yourself. The Lord wants to multiply that, one step at a time. He trusts you, and so do I."

A big smile lit her face despite the tears, "That means a lot. I'll try!"

Dani embraced her, "You have no idea how the Lord can touch people through you, because of your compassion, sister! I think you're about to realize your calling."

Erin stepped up, looked at them, then her husband, "What did I miss?"

Dani released Fran, "Allen is grooming Fran to help him minister to the needs of this burgeoning family in Christ, 'cause he says he needs help! Andrew promised to stand with her, so she's not alone."

"*Good!* I was concerned you might be spread too thin," she pulled Allen up against her, then looked at Fran. "In my opinion, he couldn't have made a better choice. You have a heart for others, while your knowledge of scripture and intimacy with Christ gives you some protection from being deceived." Fran blushed at the praise. "By the way, did the Lord show you anything about this gathering in advance?"

"Not anything definite, just that He would meet us here. Why?"

Erin burst out laughing. "That confirms what He told me, too," Allen admitted briefly with a little smile. Fran looked pleased.

His smile went away and he turned red at Erin's next statement. "Sweet Talker, if you don't tell her the rest of it, I will!" By this time, pretty much everyone was listening to their exchange.

"You know what? Upon further consideration, I agree with you, Fran. Marrying her *was* an act of bravery!" Erin chuckled, but the way she eyed him made it clear he wasn't off the hook.

"Okay, fine! Do you remember that silly little unexplained smile I gave you over dinner last night?"

"Yeah," she replied uncertainly.

"Well, it got me in trouble when we got back here. *Nothing* I say or do escapes this woman's notice, including that!" Somebody said, "Uh-oh," amongst several amused chuckles.

"Yeah, exactly. She doesn't hurt me, but she has this way of interrogating me that takes my breath away and scatters my wits. I couldn't lie to her or keep a secret if my life depended on it! I'm not willing to share how she does it; just know it's *very* effective, okay?"

An enthralled audience listened intently, as Erin watched to see that he continued. "The invitation to this gathering had gone out. Responses indicated that *all of you* would be attending. It bowled me over! As I thought about it, another thought came to mind, *"They're coming to meet with Me, not you."* That sounded like it came from the Lord. Judging from what happened today, I'd say it's confirmed now." There were several nods of agreement.

"Fran hears from God as I do," he clued in those around them. "Twice now, she has mentioned what He told her, which confirmed what He shared with me." He focused on the waitress again, "As our gaze met across the table, I wondered if you'd be confirming what He had just said, once again. The thought made me smile, which is the story behind my goofiness. Sorry if I caused any confusion," he mumbled.

"So that's what happened!" Fran laughed. "Thanks for making him 'fess up, Erin."

She touched his chin and made sure he saw her grin. "This was fun, but I didn't do it to embarrass him, guys. The way the Lord uses him like He just did makes him seem incredible to us, but I know my husband. The *last* thing he'd ever want is to be put on a pedestal." He looked up at her sharply. She was right about that!

"You all need to see how human he is, too. It's Christ operating in and through him that blows us away. He *needs* our love and support, too. He is enlisting Fran's help to guide us in following Christ because he can only stretch himself so far!"

"Both are mighty in Him but full of self-doubts, tending to second-guess anything they do that's out of the ordinary. In a way, they are the most vulnerable among us! Keep that in mind, okay? Never let them forget how much we love them, as well as how we value their help."

That drew applause, and put a lump in his throat. The tears were flowing for Fran again, but Andrew put an arm around her shoulders and drew her to his side. Denise took her hand, giving it a squeeze.

The next thing he knew, Laurie glommed onto him. He

never saw her coming! She was telling him how she loved him, which brought him to tears, too. Emily followed, then Alissa. Erin held him close after that. Dani laid a hand on his shoulder, letting him know she was near. He covered it with his own. Their affection overwhelmed him, and rendered him speechless!

Reina and Teresa were both in tears -- he didn't know why. A look passed between Ted and Liz, then he told them, "I grew up in church, same as Liz. We never saw anything like this! We were taught to love one another, that it will perfect us in Christ Jesus. Congregants exert themselves with efforts to show care for each other, but for you people, it's effortless! What makes you so different, such a family?"

They all looked toward Allen. He had a tough time talking, still choked up, but managed a few words, "Testimonies… bring us together, exalting Jesus. He binds us together in our brokenness. Let's share them with our new brethren. Win, Pam, you want to go first?"

The request animated them. They did so, eagerly. As they spoke, it was as though they settled into their niche, gained a sense of belonging. The newcomers soaked it in, amazed at what God had done for them. The Holy Spirit bore witness to their words, so hearing it again refreshed the rest of the group, even those who had heard it before.

When they finished, Fran related hers. Several were in tears over what she had endured, applauding when she came to the end. So it went through the afternoon, as one after another shared intimate details of where they came from to obtain restoration in the Lord. It bonded the two families to them. They came to realize how they were connecting to them as evening fell.

Alma remarked to Liz, "I never attended a church, but if I had heard they were like this, I might have. Who needs a membership when you fall in love with the people there?"

Liz shook her head, her eyes still wet from some of the

things she had heard. "No church I've ever seen resembles this. It's beautiful! I don't want to go home," she chuckled and sniffled.

"Well, then we have a problem," Erin deadpanned. "I don't have enough beds for everyone to stay overnight!" That brought laughter.

"You don't need one for me," Reina declared. "I'm going home to sleep in my own bed!"

Before anyone left, they took a minute to thank God for His graciousness, also offering up a prayer for Evelyn's salvation, healing, and relief from pain. Laurie thanked everyone for doing so. Erik approached her, saying something resulting in a huge dimpled grin. He handed her his ball cap.

She looked at Erin and Allen. "You guys got a pen I can borrow? Erik wants my autograph!"

Erin started describing where to find one in the office, but Allen dug into his pocket to produce two short pens and a marker he carried, out of habit. "Take your pick," he offered. At Erik's preference, she took the marker, then wrote on the bill, "I believe in you, Erik! Laurie Parcille XOXO." He was thrilled, proudly displaying it to his family.

"You have a fan," her dad observed as she returned his marker.

She giggled, "I guess I do."

He leaned his head against hers, "He isn't the only one, you know." She responded with a laugh and a quick hug.

CHAPTER 31

Reina and Teresa were still together when they approached Erin and Allen. Guillermo joined them. Carlos and Juanita also made their way over.

Reina gave both a big hug, "My family has come to know Jesus, experiencing liberty and unity in a way I thought impossible until *you two* came into our lives. He set us free and gathered us into His arms, but you were instrumental in how He did it. The two of you have a place in my heart forever! I mean that!"

"In all our hearts," Carlos expounded, bringing multiple nods.

"Including mine," Teresa spoke up. "Allen, you blow me away, how God uses you to direct, comfort, and exhort us, also teaching us from His word. Erin, you have gone from being a lump of coal, an entrepreneur whose focus was turning a profit, to becoming a dazzling diamond shining in her own right! Christ's love shines out of you through a thousand different facets. Your husband couldn't fulfill his calling the way he does without you. Your hard strength and tender care keep him going. We're learning what a wife should be by watching you, you know!"

"Well, thank you!" Erin said, somewhat bashfully. "That means a lot since I never had a mother to model or teach me what to do."

Juanita giggled, "*I'm* taking notes! I happen to know some others are, too."

Allen put his arm around Erin and stole a kiss, to the amusement of those around them. "Genie, you can't go wrong, loving me the way you do. You humble me without even trying!" A lovely grin was his reward.

Gui stepped forward to embrace him, "You're my hero, Allen! I didn't even know I needed help until the day I met you. You hooked me up with Jesus, the One who set me free. Both of you are awesome! Erin, you don't happen to have another sweet Mexican girl like my sister here who can kick my butt and love me like that, do you?" That gave them all a hard laugh.

"Afraid not, Gui, not one who loves Jesus," she replied. "Let me point out, though, that if race isn't critical to your search for love, maybe you should get to know Denise." His eyes went wide. Teresa and Juanita went "Oooo!" "She seems very sweet to me, and Stefanie is teaching her and Fran to kick butt!"

He turned to direct a curious glance her way. She didn't notice.

"Gui," Allen got his attention, "someone at the wedding suggested your honey glaze might have value to beekeepers. Have you looked into it?"

"No, not yet," he replied.

"I think you should. God could bless you financially, enabling you to be a blessing to others. You would have *so much fun* in that role while furthering the Lord's work in setting people free from sin and bondage, like He did for you. Who knows, you might even help some more stodgy Methodists get filled with the Holy Spirit!"

He gave a belly laugh that nearly doubled him over, "You figured that out, then?"

"Your thumbs-up gave it away," he chuckled.

"I love that it worked! I'll check into it, Allen. See you guys later." As the rest of them said goodnight, he bee-lined toward Denise and began talking to her.

"He's definitely not gay anymore," Carlos grinned. They were smiling as they left, though Teresa detoured to visit with Alissa's family before she followed. The men had a conversation going, while the women had congregated to have a lively discussion with frequent looks their way. Whatever they were talking about caught the interest of the kids, who had moved in close. They seemed to be questioning Dani, smiling with amusement. Andrew was still shadowing Fran. His laughter drew everyone's attention.

When they noticed, Carol addressed Erin, "Your... occupation... is so extraordinary, we're having some trouble wrapping our heads around it. It's not that we don't believe you – we do – but... How does it all work?"

The wrestlers thought it was funny. Erin patiently explained the workings of her business. Tom asked about financial returns. He was impressed at Erin's business knowledge and the answers she provided. She led everyone on a tour of the studio, showing how recordings were made as matches took place on the mats there.

Ted looked uncomfortable as Liz showed an inordinate amount of interest in the techniques the ladies used to force bigger, sometimes stronger opponents to repeatedly submit. Hearing Stef would be training Fran and Denise in their version of self-defense, his wife expressed she would like to join them. As Erin said that could be arranged, Ted sidled up to her man. Attempting to speak quietly, he garnered unwanted attention when Erin fell silent, probably due to curiosity.

"Allen, you married one of these fighting women. How

does that work?" When he realized his query was heard by the others, he flushed with embarrassment. "I'll admit it, okay? I'm worried. I'm fairly fit, but not like she is, even though she's petite. She's *very* competitive and stronger than she looks. If she learns ways to hurt me, I'm worried she'll enjoy doing it!"

She snorted. Their sons looked surprised. After a glance at Erin, he addressed Liz directly, "Has Ted ever hurt you, intentionally?"

Shaking her head, she told him, "No. He's really gentle. I admired how he handled the boys when they were small, but I had to roughhouse with him *a lot*, to get him to quit treating me like I was made of porcelain! It *really* annoyed me."

"So you had to convince him he wouldn't hurt you?"

"Exactly!"

"Going by what he just said, I think you made your point." She thought it over, and seemed pleased. "Now I think he could use some reassurance you won't hurt him, either."

"I-I... he should know that!"

"How? Has it ever come up, between you?"

"Uh... no. But still..."

He grimaced, "Liz, I can't speak for Ted, but I can try to put myself in his shoes. I'm getting older. My body doesn't work as well as it once did. My wife is very physically fit, challenges me as fiercely as ever, and kind of gets a kick out of it. Now she might get fight training to once and for all swing the balance of power in her favor.

"That's never happened before! Will she show me the same tenderness I showed her, or will my weakness provoke contempt? Unless she tells me what she's thinking and feeling, I don't know what to expect. It's a very insecure place to be!"

Win was looking at Pam, plainly thinking. Hans and Alma shared an expression like this whole topic was pure silliness.

"For some couples, where the status quo is never challenged, this discussion borders on the ridiculous, but for some of us, it's a fact of life. *Fear* has no place in marriage. The Word says, *"Men, honor your wife as the weaker vessel"*, but our marriages require *we consistently choose to honor one another*. The tougher mate has no right to hurt his or her partner. Christ holds us accountable!"

"Ted, Erin took my measure the first time we met, and knew she was more than a match for me physically. That scripture is the first we ever discussed. She took issue with it as an unbeliever but allowed me to explain it wasn't meant to be sexist. It sets a precedent in the household: *abuse is unacceptable.* Whichever partner is stronger has a responsibility to make the spouse feel safe. Erin declared the principle a thing of beauty, and took it to heart instantly."

"She wasn't satisfied, though, until *I* knew she was the stronger of us. She kept testing herself against me in little ways, playfully, until she made me certain of it. The realization scared me! I loved her so much I couldn't bear to leave her, so I took a chance and bared my heart. I found out, thank the Lord, she never meant to scare me. She was *proud* of her strength and skills, just intent on showing me what she could do."

"That made sense." He looked toward Liz, "She laid my fears to rest, promising I would always be safe with her. Since she didn't need me to be gentle, instead being careful how she handles me, I decided to give her my trust. That's the weaker vessel's contribution to the union, similar to how we trust in Christ. Erin *treasures* my trust and has never betrayed it. She constantly honors me in doing so."

"She could enforce her will on me, if she wanted. She chooses not to, for my sake. If she did, it would hinder her prayers, according to scripture. Her self-restraint honors the

Lord. He Himself instructed her to comfort me. It pleased her to embrace His command joyfully! She's CRAZY good at it, too!" That brought chuckles, with a laugh from Erin.

"You see how the Lord uses me, under her care. I was wounded, just awaiting the end of my days until she came along, yet now I have blossomed to become fruitful for Him. Do you see any evidence I am abused?"

There was amused head-shaking. Andrew spoke, "I don't, Allen, and I'm trained to look for that kind of thing."

"Thanks. You're right. Erin is one of the best things ever to happen to me! I thank God for her constantly. More important than the balance of power in a marriage is that both partners are in submission to Christ! If they respect God, regarding each other as His provision of companionship for them alone, then either doing harm to the other is unthinkable! It's too much like hurting yourself!"

Liz addressed Erin, "I've always been a tomboy, played rough, and liked to be respected for it. Being small, I got used to proving myself. I guess I have a bit of a chip on my shoulder. "Feisty" is a description I've earned repeatedly. I do tend to push my husband around to get a rise from him. He's a better nurturer than I am, truthfully."

She looked his way, "I really admire that about you, honey. I *like* to tussle, as you know." He nodded. "I take it seriously, too. If I can get the upper hand legitimately, over your honest resistance… well, that will be a thrilling moment for me! It *will* change things for us, but I swear before God as my witness, you have nothing to fear from me! This red-headed Irish girl just finds joy in taking you on, that's all!"

She took his hand with a smile, and turned back to Erin, "It was exciting, hearing other women were scrappy like me and used to winning! I like that idea; besides, it made me feel a little less freaky. I want training if you don't mind, but I'd also like to visit with you more. Hopefully, you can coach me to reward his trust the way you have with Allen. Your relationship inspires me!"

"Could we talk about something else?" Conrad wondered. "There are things about our parents we'd be happier not hearing, if you can understand that!" That drew resounding agreement from the other kids, and laughing acknowledgment from the rest.

"We'll talk later," Erin promised.

CHAPTER 32

There was a snort from Eli as he shook his head, "Strong women!" Disbelieving expressions answered him from the wrestlers, but before anyone spoke, Laurie reached into a small chest of drawers, pulled out a horseshoe, and gave it to him.

Puzzled, he asked, "What's this for?"

"Something to remember me by," she said brightly. "Do you like it?"

"I don't get it. A horseshoe?" Absently he tested it, discovering it was definitely solid. Erin and her girls grinned, knowing what would happen next.

"Oh, can I see it a moment?" He handed it back, confused. "Do you ever play this game, Eli?"

"Huh-uh, not since I was little."

Hunching some, her arms seemed to expand as she exerted pressure on the object in several pumping motions. Eyes went wide, watching as the ends moved closer together until they touched! With a dimpled grin, she extended it back to the young man. His eyes looked like they might pop out!

"Well, if you decide to play again sometime, I recommend you *don't* use this one. It would be hard to score a ringer with it, now!"

Erik applauded in delight. His sister joined in, then the rest, laughing. Conrad clapped his brother on the back, who held the gift while staring at Laurie in shock.

"Bro, looks like we know some *really* strong women. You've got the proof in your hands!"

Eli was speechless, finally breaking into a sheepish grin. She extended her hand, her eyes sparkling mischievously.

He clasped it, mumbling, "Sorry. I spoke out of turn."

"So it's a good keepsake? You'll remember me now?"

He chuckled, "Laurie, I am *never* going to forget this, or you!"

She stepped forward to kiss his cheek, "Good!" He blushed.

It made for a light-hearted end to the visit. The two new families left a couple of minutes later. Hans and Alma cast several appraising looks at the wrestlers, even at Liz. Allen got the impression perhaps they thought the earlier conversation wasn't so ridiculous, after all!

When they were gone, the ladies cracked up laughing. Andrew, Win, and Allen were the only guys left. They couldn't help laughing along with them. Laurie's brilliant response to Eli's chauvinism was congratulated repeatedly. She soaked it up with a good-natured grin, and told them seeing that shocked look on a guy's face never gets old!

Denise ribbed Andrew, "How about it, big fellow? Can you do that?"

He laughed, "I don't know. I never tried. Even if I could, though, I wouldn't do it here and now. Laurie deserves her accolades. I won't take any share of that!"

He stood firmly by his assertion when the gymnast generously offered him another horseshoe. Allen was impressed at his determination to respect her accomplishment. He wasn't the only one. Laurie gave Andrew a big hug, resulting in a bigger grin.

"You did good, girl," he told her, then pinned Erin with his gaze. "When you put me in my place, how come I didn't get off that easy?"

It cracked everyone up. Erin replied, "Because you're not just a mouthy teen. *You* should have known better! Besides, I can't bend horseshoes, so I had to make my point another way. It stuck, didn't it?"

A booming laugh was his response, "Yeah, it did! You got me there."

They began to discuss what to do about dinner. Something light sounded good after the cookout earlier. Sandwiches were mentioned, but Pam won them over with an offer to whip up a stirfry, something she had grown up with. As she rose to go to the kitchen, with Fran and Emily volunteering to help, Win caught her hand. She stopped to see why.

"Allen, I want to say thank you for calling on us first to share our testimony. What you said about it binding us together was right on!" Pam nodded seriously. "It's the first time since receiving Christ we felt like we *contributed*, did something that mattered. We needed that. We feel like we belong with you now, or at least I do, though Pam and I haven't had time to talk. Am I speaking for you, too?" he looked up at her.

Her voice was husky, "Like you're reading my mind, Win. I'm not sure I would have thought to say so, though. It wasn't like we were just reciting an experience; it felt like we were sharing a part of ourselves with everyone. You said it, it mattered." She looked at Allen with sincerity, "Thank you for the opportunity, for calling on us and *including* us."

He got up and walked over to hug each of them. "There's nothing like serving our Lord, is there?" Win had risen at his approach. Both heartily agreed. There were some sniffles in the room. "You two *are* a part of us, as much as we are united in Him. Don't ever let the Devil trick you into thinking otherwise, okay?" They agreed, smiling.

They visited into the evening, enjoying each other's company until he started *yawning* again. It became such a source of amusement he invited everyone to go home, threatening to go to bed, rather than continue being laughed at! Erin admonished him he was being cranky. He told everyone with a laugh if they could come back tomorrow, he'd try to do better. By this time, the yawning had spread enough to convince them to clear out!

ABOUT THE AUTHOR

L. A. Goodyear is a jack of all trades. He has worked in lumber yards, a donut shop, warehouses, truck driving, cashiering - even participated in laser surgery! A veteran of the U.S. Navy, his most recent occupation was that of a caregiver for the developmentally disabled.

He loves to laugh and get others laughing, but most of all he loves talking about the Lord Jesus he serves. Obeying and spending time with Him is a joy he'd share with everyone, if he could! He sees ministry as a matter of meeting needs whenever enabled to do so by the power of God, rather than an occupation to earn a livelihood, and is acutely aware he will give account for his faithfulness.

L. A. maintains a blog, *thefoolishnessofgod.com*, where he expounds on scripture and sometimes airs his thoughts on matters of interest. He can be reached at *thefoolishnessofgod@yahoo.com*. It amuses him to tell people he writes foolishness!